BE MY LOVE

A Walker Island Romance, Book 1

Lucy Kevin

BE MY LOVE
A Walker Island Romance, Book 1
© 2015 Lucy Kevin

Come for a visit to Walker Island where you'll find stunning Pacific Northwest ocean views, men too intriguing to resist...and five beautiful, close-knit sisters who are each about to find their one true love.

After four years on the Seattle mainland, when Hanna Walker returns to Walker Island to make a documentary about the infamous Peterson-Walker feud from the early 1950s, she's shocked to realize that passions still run high. Especially when it comes to Joel Peterson, the one man who is totally off-limits...but that she's never been able to stop dreaming about.

The last thing Joel wants is for Hanna to dredge up the past, but when he realizes she's determined to follow through with her documentary no matter what, he knows he has no choice but to join her. Despite vowing to hold back his growing feelings for her, as Joel works with Hanna to unravel the mystery of what really happened between their two families, he soon begins to see that love is an unstoppable force...and that sometimes two people are meant to be.

CHAPTER ONE

Hanna Walker stood on the deck of the ferry, enjoying the spray kicking up from the ocean and the wind whipping at her hair as she worked to keep her video camera steady against the roll of the boat. As the butternut-squash shape of the island came into view, she shifted her focus from the ocean and blue sky to Walker Island.

Home.

She'd spent four years at the University of Washington in Seattle while she worked toward her film degree, but the island still felt like home every time she returned. She hadn't been able to get away from school and her part-time job nearly as often as she'd wanted to over the years, but Hanna could always picture the Walker crew clearly in her head.

Her grandmother, Ava, an incredibly beautiful woman at eighty, running her dancing studio with the energy of a woman half her age.

Her father, Tres, "losing" his glasses on top of his head at least three times each day as he graded papers from his English students and planned one of his school trips. Her oldest sister, Emily, making a huge breakfast for everyone in the house before she headed off for another busy day as a Guidance Counselor at the island's combined junior high and high school. Her second-oldest sister, Rachel, who worked for an insurance agency, keeping track of at least three things at once while her five-year-old daughter, Charlotte, ran happy circles around her. Her middle sister, Paige, always elegant in a leotard and tights, teaching dance in the studio with Grams. Only her sister Morgan, who at twenty-five was just two years older than Hanna, wouldn't be on the island. Instead, she'd be shooting her popular makeover segment in New York City. Or, possibly, working her magic with makeup brushes in Los Angeles or Paris to make some movie star look stunning before they went off to a premiere and posed with smiles on their faces so that the photographers could get their shots.

Just the way I should be shooting right now, Hanna reminded herself. She turned her attention back to the water just in time to film a whale surfacing with her calf, the spray from her blowhole shooting a good fifteen feet into the air. Hanna caught every detail of the droplets, using the sun at an angle to capture the brief rainbow that sprang up in the fine mist. She spotted more whales from the same pod moving along beside the others and tracked them until the mother of the calf dove again, down into the ocean depths.

The island would be at its busiest for the next few months, filled with both tourists and the research teams who came from all around the world to study the whale migrations. Summer was one of the most vibrant times of the year to be on Walker Island, apart from the winter holidays. The only downside to coming home over the summer was that her father was usually off in Europe on a school trip, teaching kids about the origins of great literature.

Hanna searched the water for more whales, but they'd disappeared for the time being. And maybe that was a good thing, given that she could practically hear Professor Karlson talking to her as if he were beside her on the boat.

"I know you can frame a shot, Hanna. Now it's time to show me—and yourself, as well— something with some heart in it."

She'd lost track of the number of times she'd tried to dig deeper only to have him tell her that she still wasn't quite reaching far enough inside the emotional core of what she was filming. Unfortunately, the last time he'd said it to her had been when she'd applied for the University's master's program in documentary filmmaking.

"If you want to get into the program, you have to do more than show me you can hold a camera, or even tell a story. You have to show me your heart, Hanna. That's the hard part, but it's also the difference between a real documentary maker and

everyone else."

She'd been lucky that he'd even given her a provisional acceptance into the graduate level program. Acceptance that was contingent on her showing him that she could rise to the challenge to create a documentary that truly moved her, so that it, in turn, would move others, too.

That was when Hanna knew it was time to go home to Walker Island. Because if Professor Karlson wanted to see something from the heart, Hanna had to go where her heart *was.*

She found a couple of facing seats on the ferry that weren't occupied, then set up her camera on one of them and sat opposite. Morgan was the only Walker sister who regularly went in front of the camera for her makeup segments, but Hanna had been a part of enough other students' film projects over the years to feel fairly comfortable being filmed. Behind her, there would be just enough of the ocean and the island for the viewer to see that she was on a ferry boat in the Pacific Northwest.

"I'm on my way home to Walker Island, and before we get into the harbor I'd like to give a quick history of the island." Hanna knew she would probably have to cut parts of this out, but she could always edit in some better images to go with the sound if she needed to toward the end of her project.

"There have been native settlements on the island for at least three hundred years, and there are many interesting and important archaeological finds from Snohomish settlements. In 1921, my great grandfather William Walker lost his family farm north of Seattle. Utterly despondent, he sailed off into the ocean, intending never to come back or to farm again. But when his boat washed up on the shores of Walker Island—and he found varieties of wild blueberries and blackberries that were twice as plump and flavorful as any they'd grown on the mainland—he took that as a sign that he should try again. Not just with farming, but to rebuild the Walker family, as well. It turned out to be a great decision, because with its own microclimate like many of the Pacific Northwest islands, his farms were able to survive both the Great Depression and the Dust Bowl. The major problem my great grandfather ran into was how to best transport the berries off of the island. Fortunately, this was solved with the help of a local mussel-farming family, the Petersons, who also ended up running the largest shipping company on Walker Island, and the island's ferries."

Hanna continued to tell the story she knew by heart to the camera. "My grandfather, William Walker II, who was always more interested in education than in running a berry-growing business, built the combined junior high and high school on the island. He was also engaged to marry the Petersons' only daughter, Poppy, which would have cemented both the business and personal relationship between the two island families."

Hanna had done this ferry ride so many times between Seattle and Walker Island that as they rounded the southern tip of the island, she knew the ferry captain was about to make his announcement for everyone to return to their car on the deck below the seating area. In the sixty remaining seconds she had before his announcement boomed through the ship's speakers, she said, "This documentary is going to follow the history—and ramifications—of what happened next. Namely, the engagement being cancelled, the berry business being sold to one of the largest jam makers in the United States, and a feud between the Petersons and Walkers that has lasted for decades."

Just as the captain's announcement came, Hanna picked up the camera and headed down to the pedestrian waiting area on the deck to get a long shot of the harbor as the ferry docked.

A few minutes later, after Hanna hopped off the boat, a man wearing a "Walker Island Whale Watching Tours" hat smiled at her. "Hi, Hanna. It's good to see you back on the island. Your grandmother has been talking about your return for weeks."

Jonas had been giving tours for so many years that Hanna knew him quite well. "It's great to be back," she said with a smile. "How's Jenny doing?"

"Great." His grin widened. "We just had a little girl named Madison." He quickly pulled out a picture of the cute baby which Hanna, and everyone else in line, oohed and aahed over.

"She's just lovely, Jonas. Congratulations."

As she stepped away to let everyone get on with buying their whale watching tickets, she marveled at just how nice it was to be back home. As much as she loved Seattle, there was no place quite like Walker Island.

Knowing everyone in her family was likely to be busy with work for the next couple of hours, she decided to get some good B-roll footage of the island while the weather was so clear. She filmed a small team of scientists about to set off for the tide pools, and one of the women who had come in several times to give guest lectures at the high school recognized Hanna and waved a hello to her. Next, she got some footage of one of the many local artists working on an oil painting of the harbor, and found herself agreeing to pose for a painting if she could carve out a few hours here and there in the coming weeks.

Once she felt that she had enough footage of a typical summer's day on Walker Island, she put down her camera to call the head of the local historical society. Benjamin Neale also ran the extremely popular ice cream stand, so she wasn't surprised to get his voicemail. "Mr. Neale, this is Hanna Walker, and I'd like to make sure that it is still okay for me to come take a look through the local archives as we had discussed a few weeks ago. I've just arrived back on the island and would appreciate a call back when you get a chance."

Hanna was just ending the call when she felt

a small hand tugging at her pants. A little boy who looked to be around her niece's age had broken away from the family of tourists he was with and was looking up at her.

"Are you famous?"

Hanna smiled back at him. "Why would you think I'm famous?"

"Everyone here seems to know you," the boy said, "so you must be famous. Plus, you have those pink streaks in your hair like a rock star."

"I'm not famous," Hanna told him with a grin. "My sister, Morgan, is a little famous, but only because she's on TV sometimes. Mostly, though, people just know me because I'm a Walker."

"Wow," the boy said in a clearly awed voice, "so since this is Walker Island, does this mean it's *yours*?"

Hanna laughed. "No, it doesn't quite work like that."

In fact, she reflected as the boy ran back to his family to give them the full scoop, it didn't work *at all* like that. Her great grandfather might have had the whole island to himself for a little while, but all her life they'd been just like any other family, doing the same things everyone else on the island did to get by.

The Walkers had never shied away from hard work. Her older sisters had taken part in the berry picking when they were all younger, and she'd had to work her way through college, the same as everyone else. Just because their great grandfather was the first settler on the island, it wasn't like they were royalty or anything.

Still, whenever Hanna wondered what it would have been like to grow up in a town that wasn't named after her family and that wasn't so small most people knew her by sight, she knew one thing for certain: It wouldn't be home.

Just then, her phone rang and she was thrilled to see that Mr. Neale had found a moment or two between ice cream scoops to get back to her.

"Hanna, hello. I've been meaning to get back to you about your visit to the archives. I'm afraid that there has been a bit of a…" He cleared his throat before continuing. "Well, it's a bit of a hitch regarding your project."

"A hitch?" Hanna didn't like the sound of that. Ava, her grandmother, was going to be the heart of the documentary, but the interviews with her needed to be backed up by proper research. Names and dates. Documents. Important elements that would give the piece the depth it would need to win her a place in the graduate filmmaking program. "What sort of hitch?"

Again, Mr. Neale cleared his throat in obvious discomfort. "I'm afraid one of our committee members has blocked your application to use the archives."

"Why would someone do that?" Hanna had assumed that the whole process of applying for archival access was just a formality.

"I'm afraid I can't speak for the committee member, Ms. Walker."

"Do you know how long this glitch will take to iron out?" she asked in what she hoped was a patient voice. "Because I really only have the summer to finish this documentary. And I absolutely *have* to finish this documentary."

"I'm sorry," he replied, and to be fair he did sound sorry. "But Joel Peterson was quite clear that he doesn't want you to have access to the archives for a documentary. In any case, I have to get back to work now. It looks like there's a party of kids coming in. Take care, Hanna."

As she slipped her phone back into her pocket, she tried to make sense of what the historical society's chairman had just told her. Why would Joel want to keep her out of the archives?

Joel had been her sister Rachel's age at school, which made him seven years older than Hanna. She could remember sitting on the sidelines of a school football game, watching him play. He'd been the quarterback, and it always seemed that when he had the ball, no one could touch him. On top of that, he'd been the best looking boy she'd ever seen.

She'd seen him from time to time around the island over the years since high school, but she suspected he still only knew her as Rachel's kid sister. They'd certainly never spoken as adults.

Clearly, it was time to correct that. She could go home and get settled in, but it would be better to find Joel and get this mess straightened out first. Once they actually talked, she was sure that his refusal to let her into the archives would turn out to be no more than a mistake.

Besides, she had to admit, she was interested in seeing how the handsome boy from the football field had turned out.

CHAPTER TWO

"Good morning, Margaret," Joel said as he walked into his office at Peterson Shipping Company. Margaret had been his father's secretary before him, and Joel had known her for nearly thirty years, back when he was just starting to learn the basics of the business that he'd always known he would inherit. "What do we have on tap for today?"

"There are a few messages for you to look through on your desk before your meeting with Frank Williams from the Mussel Farmers' Union at eleven. And if you don't mind me saying," she said with a fond smile, "your tie looks great with that shirt."

Margaret had given it to him for his birthday a few weeks back, and though wearing a tie always made him feel like he had a noose around his neck, Joel smiled back. "Thanks, Margaret. And please let me know when Frank arrives."

He stepped into his office, which had been his father's office and his grandfather's before that. Joel had kept the framed newspaper pictures of the two of them collecting industry awards, along with the big solid cedar wood desk by the window that had a clear view out over the water. Joel swung the door shut behind him, and only then did he reach up to loosen the tie so that he could breathe again.

"If we don't set a standard," his father had often said, *"how can we expect people to respect us?"*

Peterson Shipping wasn't the biggest shipping company in the world, but the company still needed constant attention. As a child, Joel hadn't been able to understand why his father had to work so many Saturdays. Now he knew.

The ocean didn't care what day of the week it was, and a skipper running into trouble around the island didn't either.

Joel began to read through his emails and messages. The ones from the boat skippers came first, of course, because if you didn't look after the boats and their crews, then you didn't deserve to run a shipping business. Simple as that.

Well, perhaps not exactly *simple.* Nothing around the island was simple. There were usually at least three or four complaints waiting for him. The most pressing complaint today was about a rogue operator, which he'd have to see the harbor master about. Of course, the upside was that he might actually get out of the office and down to the harbor at some point.

When Joel was a kid sailing small boats around the island on school holidays with his father, running Peterson shipping had seemed like the best job in the world. Yet the truth was that every season, Joel spent less time on boats and more doing paperwork and sending emails.

He was beginning to read through the minutes from the last meeting of the Mussel Farmers' Union when one final message from Margaret slid out. He saw the name first—Hanna Walker—before seeing that Benjamin Neale had called, again, regarding her request to go through the local historic archives.

"Hanna Walker wants to make a documentary film about what happened between your family and hers," was what Benjamin had told him a few weeks ago. *"She wants access to the archives. Now, none of the rest of the society board have any objections—"*

"No," Joel had said. *"Absolutely not."*

And that had been that, he'd assumed. Yet now there was another message about her. What was the youngest Walker sister trying to do with her documentary? Open up old wounds? Reignite old arguments?

Joel had no intention of doing either. The past needed to stay in the past.

Her grandfather had turned his back on the Peterson-Walker merger and then his great aunt Poppy had taken her life. Why would anyone want to rake up all that?

The only thing that made sense was that Hanna obviously planned to use whatever skills she had with a video camera to reinvent the past. Wasn't it true that people tended to believe what they saw on a TV screen over the truth? A few truths, a few lies, and suddenly the Walker family would come out of the whole mess looking far better than they had actually been. With access to the archives, Hanna would likely be able to put together enough information to make whatever mangled version of the truth she wanted to sell seem believable.

Joel couldn't risk that. He *wouldn't* risk that.

He owed it to his family not to.

He'd known most of her older sisters from school, but his memories of Hanna were as a little shadow trailing behind Emily, Rachel, Paige and Morgan. Not, of course, that Joel had ever had much to do with the Walkers at school. He was a Peterson, after all.

Shaking his head, he had just re-focused on the meeting minutes regarding mussel seeding ratios when he heard Margaret arguing with someone outside the door.

"I'm sorry, but Mr. Peterson can't be disturbed right now. He has a meeting soon—"

"I understand," another woman said, "but if he's not with anyone right now, this will only take a few minutes. We just have a small misunderstanding to straighten out."

Joel didn't have time to straighten his tie before a woman pushed open the door to his office. Small and fine-boned, she was incredibly beautiful, albeit in a slightly unconventional way. Her blonde hair was streaked with light pink highlights, and her eyes shone out, blue and fierce from beneath her bangs. Even in cargo pants and a denim jacket it was obvious that she had a gorgeous figure.

As a high school quarterback, the son of the local shipping magnate, and then the director of the family business, Joel had had his share of relationships with good looking women. But there was something uniquely attractive about the way this woman strode over to his desk like nothing in the world was going to stop her from getting what she wanted.

Of course, by that point, two other things had become pretty obvious, both of which should have dampened the attraction Joel had felt in that first glance. The first was that she was probably only in her early twenties, which was far too young for him. But it was the second that was far more important.

She was a Walker.

Hanna Walker.

She might have been the youngest Walker sister, but she was no longer a little girl. Not even close.

"Oh, wow," she said, her eyes widening as she stopped moving closer to stare at him. "You would look just *great* on camera."

"Hanna—"

"You recognized me." She sounded surprised.

"I wasn't sure you would. I've grown up."

Yes, he thought, *you certainly have.* This close, he could smell the fresh scent of the sea on her and guessed that she must have only just come over on the ferry. He knew she was here to convince him to let her into the archives, but just looking at her beautiful face scrambled up his brain cells so badly that before he could put them back in order and let her know he wasn't going to change his mind, she was moving closer...and scrambling his insides up more and more with every step she took.

"I just spoke to Mr. Neale, who told me that you'd said I couldn't have access to the archives, but I figured that couldn't be right. I mean, why would you do that? And since he's very busy with everyone who wants ice cream today, I thought I'd come here and talk to you directly. And you know, you really *would* look great on camera. Maybe we could do a segment in the documentary with you talking about how the Peterson family is doing now, a couple of generations after the big feud? And we could also include a few shots of mussel farming, because though I know it isn't totally relevant to our families' stories, it is a really big part of the island culture and industry." Barely pausing for breath, she added, "So if you could let Mr. Neale know it was just a slight mix up, that would be great. And it would be even better if you could talk to him today, because I need to get to work on my documentary immediately so that I can edit it together and submit it before the end of the summer."

Joel was, frankly, stunned by Hanna's passion. He'd hoped that her interest in the Walker-Peterson feud would be fleeting. But as she began to move even closer—close enough that he could smell the lavender scent of her shampoo in addition to the sea spray on her skin—he realized he had to stop this here and now. All of this.

"There is no mix up." He pushed away from his desk, and made himself move across the room, away from all of her incredible beauty and passion. "I'm not going to give you access to the historical archives."

"But why?"

How, he wondered, could she be this genuinely surprised by his response? "Hasn't your grandmother told you why?"

For the first time since entering his office, she looked a little unsure. "I haven't told Grams about it quite yet," Hanna admitted. "The interview with her will be one of the main features of the documentary, and if I told her what I was doing too soon, it might spoil her natural reaction. It's really important with documentaries to get people's real reactions."

"Oh, trust me," Joel told her, "once you bring this up with your grandmother, you'll get a real reaction. Surely, you know the details of the island scandal, don't you?" Details of a feud that had been drummed into Joel's head from as far back as he could remember.

"Some of them," she replied, "although I won't know everything until I've had a chance to look through the archives properly."

"No," he said again. "And once you speak with your grandmother, I'm certain you'll understand why I can't support your documentary project."

Before Hanna could try to argue her case again, Margaret opened the door. "Joel, Frank Williams is here for your meeting. Do you need him to wait a few minutes?"

Hanna spoke first. "No, that's okay. I need to go let my family know I'm back home." Scrupulously polite now, and in direct contrast to the way she had barged in earlier, she said, "Thank you for your time, Joel."

When she turned and walked out with her spine straight and her head held high, Joel couldn't help but admire her beauty yet again. Working to shake her vibrant image out of his head as he shook hands with the head of the Mussel Farmers' Union, Joel did his best to focus on the meeting so that he could understand the changes they wanted. But all the while his brain was somewhere else entirely.

Still thinking about Hanna...

CHAPTER THREE

"Hanna?" Ava Walker stepped out of the front door just as Hanna was about to head inside. "When did you get back, darling? We would have come down to the ferry to meet you."

There were those who said that Ava had been a real beauty in her youth. Hanna always thought they had it wrong. Her grandmother was beautiful *now.* She kept herself in great shape with regular exercise and healthy food and still moved with the poise of a dancer. Her bright blue eyes still had plenty of fire in them, too.

"I came in on the two o'clock, but I didn't want to interrupt any of you when you were working. Plus, it's such a beautiful day that I wanted to get some footage of town."

She'd had a wonderful time in town...that is, until her run-in with Joel at the Peterson Shipping offices. Hanna had always been happy to get back to the island during school breaks, but all she could think about right then was how Joel had flat out *ruined* her plans for the documentary.

"Hanna, what is it?" Ava asked, reaching out to take hold of her hand. "You look so upset."

"No, it's..." Hanna shook her head. If her grandmother was on the way out, then she didn't have enough time to go into it all. "We can talk about it later if you have to go open up the studio for your afternoon classes."

"Oh, Paige has already done that," Ava assured her. "And I'm sure she can handle things there a little longer while you tell me what's going on." Putting her arm around Hanna's waist, she said, "Come on inside."

Together, they headed through the entry and into the kitchen. The big old house that had held so many generations of Walkers wasn't a mansion, but could easily accommodate five energetic kids running around. The kitchen was the largest room in the house, with a big dining table around which the whole family could fit to eat.

Hanna wasn't surprised to see a man in a plaid shirt and jeans working beneath the sink. Michael Bennet had moved in with the Walkers for a few years as a teenager when he'd lost his parents. Hanna had always looked at him as a big brother. All of her sisters did. Well, all except Emily, who could never quite hide her emotions whenever she looked at the dark-eyed, dark-haired man who was always underfoot....

When he spotted her, Michael quickly moved

to his feet to pull her into a warm hug. "I thought we'd gotten rid of you to Seattle for good. I'm glad to see I was wrong about that."

"Does Emily know you're fiddling with her sink?" Hanna countered with a big grin as she hugged him back just as hard.

"No, but she does now," Hanna's oldest sister said from the kitchen door.

Hanna had often thought that Emily was the prettiest of them all, even if some days it seemed like she was too busy to make much of an effort. Today, she had her hair tied back, and she hadn't bothered putting on any makeup, which would have horrified Morgan's makeup-artist soul. Emily had always been so much more than a big sister, having stepped up to take care of all of them after their mother passed away.

"Welcome home, Hanna," Emily said as she also gave her a hug, before turning to Michael. "You didn't leave your crew down at Mrs. Hellman's house to come fix our sink, did you?"

"Ava asked me to have a look at it. And now," he said as he flipped the faucet up and water poured out into the sink, "you don't have to do it."

Hanna watched the play of emotions roll across her big sister's face: pleasure at being near Michael, which turned into longing for more, before Emily tamped down on all of it.

"Thank you," Emily finally said, "for fixing it just in time for me to get dinner started for everyone. Are you going to stay to eat with us?"

Michael's eyes were full of the same longing

Hanna had just seen in her sister's eyes as he watched Emily efficiently move to the fridge and pull out three bell peppers. "Only if you think you'll have enough."

Seriously, how many years were the two of them going to do this dance with each other? Frustrated by both of them, Hanna sat down with her grandmother at the kitchen table and said, "She always makes enough." When both Michael and Emily looked surprised by her tone, she immediately apologized. "I'm sorry. I didn't mean to sound snarky."

Her grandmother reached for her hand. "What is it, Hanna? What's wrong?"

She knew she'd feel better if she got everything off her chest, but at the same time, she hated spoiling things in her first few moments back home by complaining about her film...and Joel.

When she didn't immediately spill her guts, her grandmother squeezed her hand. "Whatever problems you might be having, if you'll talk to us about them, I'm sure we can put our minds together to find a way to work things out."

"Not if Joel Peterson has anything to say about it, it won't," Hanna replied with more force than she intended. "I just went to see him in his office, actually."

"You went to see the Peterson boy?" Ava said, her eyebrows raised in surprise.

"He's not a boy anymore, Grams," Emily said, putting down a plate of crackers, cheese and fruit for them to munch on before dinner. "He's the head of Peterson shipping now and is only a couple of years younger than me."

"What did Joel do to upset you so much?" Michael asked as he loaded up a cracker with two slices of sharp cheddar.

"I'm only provisionally accepted into grad school and I have to do a piece that's good enough to truly earn my spot. Something with *heart.*" Hanna resisted the urge to slam her hand onto the table top in frustration. She knew from her teenage tantrums that the Walker family table was *much* harder than her hand. "But now that Joel has blocked my access to the archives, the project I was working on is dead in the water."

"Why did you want access to the archives?" Ava asked.

Hanna thought about Joel's parting words. He'd seemed to be under the impression that her grandmother wouldn't like it when she told her what she was doing. Yet that couldn't be right, could it? The Peterson-Walker feud was all in the past now. And yet, at the same time, Hanna sensed that it was a story that needed to be told.

"I want to make a documentary on the Peterson-Walker split."

"Are you crazy?" Emily asked.

Hanna stared at her older sister in shock. *Are you crazy* was precisely the sort of thing school guidance counselors weren't supposed to say. Besides, her sister had always been so supportive. Anything Hanna needed, Emily—and the rest of her sisters—had helped her with in the past. If anything, the problem was that they sometimes tried to help too much.

"The island feud is the perfect subject for a documentary. There's history and tension, and I've got great archival sources, plus Grams is the one living person who really remembers what happened."

"Only, now Joel doesn't want you to have access to the archives," Ava gently pointed out.

"It's all for the best," Emily said as she pushed her knife into the bell pepper. "There are plenty of other things on the island that you could make a documentary about."

"Like what?" Hanna asked her sister, barely managing to keep the snark from seeping out again. "The whale migration?"

"Sure, why not?"

"I'm not interested in making a wildlife documentary," Hanna insisted. "And even if I was, I couldn't get access to the expensive cameras I'd need for that."

"Okay, then don't make it about the whales. How about the disappearance of the Snohomish from our island two hundred years ago? No one has ever done a good job of explaining what happened. You could look into the theories behind it."

"You're right," Hanna said. "Someone should definitely do a documentary about the disappearance of the Snohomish. But I'm not the right person to tell that story. Not when what I really want to do—and what I *need* to do if I'm going to have any chance of securing my spot in the graduate program—is make a film about something close to me. Something that's close to the heart of what I truly care about."

"If you really cared," Emily said, "you wouldn't go dragging Grams into this. You're kicking a hornet's nest here. And all for what? Some documentary? Do you really think people want to watch a show about some stupid family fight that belongs in the past? Are you trying to hurt people, Hanna?"

Hanna didn't think she'd seen her sister genuinely angry with her before. Occasionally exasperated, yes, but never angry. "No, of course I'm not trying to hurt anyone!" she shot back, "but—"

"Enough, both of you."

Ava didn't say it loudly, but Hanna and Emily both immediately fell silent. It was just like when they were children and Rachel and Morgan would be fighting to be the center of attention. Grams was the only one with the knack for getting them to stop. "Now, Emily, Hanna, do you two girls really want to argue?"

Hanna shook her head. Emily did the same.

"I just don't want Hanna doing something that's going to hurt you," Emily said.

"I'm not going to do that," Hanna insisted. "I just want to interview you, Grams, to find out what really happened back then and how you felt about it."

"And I want my granddaughters to be able to follow their dreams, even if it's painful." She gave each of them a small smile. "When Morgan left to pursue her career in TV off the island, I know it was very bittersweet for all of us. It hurt, not seeing her, but at least we all know that she is doing what she loves. All of you should do the things that you love."

When Emily opened her mouth to say something else, Michael gently put a hand on her arm. Whatever it was that silently passed between them had her turning her focus back to the vegetables she was cutting.

"If this documentary is a step along the path to following your dreams," Ava told her, "then I support you. Just as I know your sisters will."

"Thank you, Grams. You're the best," Hanna said as she threw her arms around her grandmother. Without the archives, she'd be missing a lot of the information, but interviewing Ava would hopefully cut through most of the problems. And she wouldn't have to worry about Joel anymore. "By the time you get back from the studio, Grams, I'll have my camera set up, and then—"

Ava held up a hand. "I want you to follow your dreams, but at the same time, I won't be able to give you the interview that you want, darling."

"Why not?"

"I made a promise a long time ago. One I can't break."

"But if I can't interview you, and I can't go

into the archives, how will I make this work?"

"You'll find a way," Ava said with utter confidence. "And maybe...well, maybe once you do make your documentary, it will finally be time that this story was told. But no matter what bumps you may hit along the road, I want you to make a promise to me to keep following your dreams, Hanna."

"Of course I will, but—"

Her grandmother stood before she could finish her sentence. "Now, I'd best be getting down to the dance studio. It's lovely to have you home." With a kiss on Hanna's cheek, Ava left.

CHAPTER FOUR

Joel wasn't in his office, but fortunately the island was small enough that it took her less than thirty minutes to find him down at the docks talking to a mussel boat captain. It immediately struck her that the docks seemed to fit him a lot better than the office had. In fact, she could easily picture him piloting a boat, the spray washing over him.

Since Hanna had her camera with her, she zoomed in on Joel until it was just his face backed by the ocean, the blue water moving in the background and the sunlight shining down on his dark hair.

"Hanna? What are you doing?"

She lowered the camera. "I was right about you," she said with a smile.

"Right about what?"

"You do look great on camera."

But instead of smiling back, Joel said, "You

shouldn't just film someone without their knowledge like that."

"I never walk away without letting them know and getting their permission to use the clip," she reassured him. "But it's usually better to film first and ask later in order to catch the real person rather than the shell most people keep around them."

"I don't keep a shell around me."

Hanna looked at his tie pointedly. The one that had been halfway off in his office. She knew men on whom a tie looked elegant, even stylish.

On Joel it looked more like a restriction.

"If you say so. In any case, I've spoken with my grandmother about the documentary and she said that she wants me to follow my dreams."

"Regardless of who it hurts?"

Joel stepped away from the edge of the dock. Behind him, the mussel boat pulled away, and Hanna thought she saw him glance back towards it almost longingly.

Was he that eager to get away from her?

Regardless, with no access to the historical sources she needed, and having been left with no main interview subject for her documentary due to a promise her grandmother had made to someone many years ago, Hanna desperately needed to change Joel's mind about the archives.

"Will you at least let me try to talk you into it?" Hanna suggested. "Maybe over coffee?"

Joel shook his head. "I have more skippers to talk to. I can't just run off to have coffee with you to discuss the archives when I have a business to run."

He was heading off briskly in the direction of another boat when Hanna darted in front of him. To get around her, he would have to swim.

"What are you so afraid of, Joel?"

"I'll tell you exactly what I'm afraid of. That you'll hurt my family with your selfish need to put together some documentary."

"Selfish?" Hanna couldn't hold back a spark of anger. "That isn't fair."

"What happened back in the fifties wasn't *fair*," Joel countered. "So I'll tell you again, I won't let you hurt my family."

"Do you really think I'd do that?" Part of her wanted to smack him for being so hard-headed. A slightly more worrying part of her wanted to kiss him. The trouble was, she suspected that whichever one she did, it wouldn't make an iota of difference to him.

"I honestly don't know what you'd do," Joel replied. "You left the island as a kid and you've come back as...as someone else. Because despite all of your assurances to the contrary, for all I know, you plan on twisting history around to make my family look bad. I can't take that risk. Not when it comes to my family. Now, why don't you step out of the way if you don't want to get wet."

He brushed past her, so close that his hand briefly brushed over hers, which immediately sent thrill bumps racing across her skin.

"Even if you won't believe that I'm not here to do a hatchet job on your family, why not at least give me *your* take on what happened?" Hanna called after him. "What will that hurt?"

The slight hitch in his step was her only clue that he was at all tempted to speak with her about his family. But it was enough for her to press forward. "I know you still need to talk to your skippers, but I did a whole degree in filmmaking. I can easily shoot a little footage on the move."

"And if you happen to fall into the water?"

"Oh, don't worry, I can swim. You won't have to get your suit wet saving me."

He frowned. "Do you really think I'd worry about my suit if you fell in?"

Well, that was a surprisingly sweet thing for him to say. "It's a nice suit," she replied even as she felt her cheeks begin to flush at the way he was staring down at her.

Before they could get too close and easy with each other, he took a step back. "All right, then. I'll tell you about what happened."

Barely holding in a victorious little cheer, she kept the camera carefully focused on him as they made their way along the docks.

"In 1951, the Petersons and the Walkers were very close. The families had been friends since the founding of the island, but by the early fifties that friendship had blossomed into something more for Poppy Peterson and William Walker II. Not only were they in love, but their marriage would also join together the two biggest businesses on the island, mussel farming for the Petersons and berry growing for the Walkers."

He reached out for her arm to help her step around a tourist who was taking a photograph of the docks. Just at the moment they made contact, he stopped speaking and what she saw in his dark eyes as he looked through the camera to her stole her breath.

Quickly drawing his hand back, he continued, saying, "The whole island was looking forward to the big wedding, and from what I've read, everyone believed the two of them were a really great couple. It was simply a bonus that their marriage would create a business merger that would be good for the local economy. Unfortunately, that was when your grandfather ruined everything by breaking off the engagement."

Through her lens, Hanna could see the flash of anger in Joel's eyes.

"He had met your grandmother in Seattle. And, somehow, she had managed to convince him that his feelings for Poppy, and everything else that had been arranged between the two families and their businesses, didn't matter. She not only persuaded him to marry her instead, but she also persuaded him to walk away from the berry business and to sell it for easy money."

By this point in Joel's version of the story, Hanna found that she was having to hold back her own spark of anger. He was being *so* unfair, believing that everything had been her grandmother's fault. But how could he know that if he'd never actually spoken to Ava about any of it? And, worse still, how could anyone ever find out the truth if her grandmother's promise precluded her from officially setting the record straight?

"My great aunt Poppy was so shamed by what the Walkers had done to her," Joel said in a low voice that rumbled with emotion, "that she purposely took a boat out without a crew in bad weather. My family has never been the same since."

Hanna instinctively turned off her camera. Both she and Joel were upset now, and it no longer felt right to keep filming.

"So there it is." His voice was clipped now, and hard. "That's what happened. Making a documentary won't change those facts. And it certainly won't change what William II and Ava did to my family."

"But what if you're not completely right about what happened or why it happened? And what about everything you left out? Because you certainly didn't mention that Grams loved Grandpa while he was alive. I saw how much they cared about one another when I was little. To go against his family's wishes like that, they must have loved each other a great deal."

Joel shook his head as if love didn't change anything. "What about how they sold the berry business? Do you think that was about love or about money?"

"Grandpa used that money to invest in building and staffing the local school, which he was always very passionate about, just like my father and sister," Hanna pointed out. "And do we know whether he gave your family a chance to buy the business or not? Do we know for sure how everyone reacted? Plus, didn't he make sure that the new owners of the company would hire locals first for berry season so that the island jobs wouldn't disappear?"

"Just like I thought, you're trying to twist things around."

"No, I'm simply asking questions. Questions I need the archives to answer, Joel." When he got that look on his face that told her he was going to refuse her request again, like any good sailor would have, she quickly changed tack. "I'm doing an interview with Milton Forsythe tomorrow morning."

"At the marine conservation offices?"

Hanna nodded. "Mr. Forsythe doesn't have much firsthand knowledge of the feud, but his father was a go-between for both of our families during all this. I'd like you to come with me."

"You would?" Surprise shifted to suspicion as he asked, "Why?"

"I really want access to those archives, Joel. And the only way I'm going to get that is if I can prove to you that you can trust me."

"You think going along with you to see Milton will do that?"

"I hope it will," Hanna said. "Come along with me to see him. See that I'm not putting words into his mouth. And that I'm being fair. If you're happy then, though, I expect to be given access to the archives."

Joel seemed thoughtful. "And if I'm not?"

"Then you obviously aren't going to change your mind, and I'll have to think of some other way to get the answers I need."

"So you won't make me a promise to leave the past alone?"

"When something is important to me, I can't just forget all about it. This documentary is happening. The only question is whether it happens with or without you."

For a moment, she thought she might have gone too far. Joel certainly looked like he might say *without*, which definitely wasn't the answer she wanted to hear.

But, thankfully, Joel finally said, "All right. I'll go with you to see Milton."

CHAPTER FIVE

Milton's place was practically a museum in its own right, filled with relics of decades in the whale watching business. Everything from a collection of shots of dorsal fins to a battered life preserver taken from a now-decommissioned boat. His living room had one of the better views on the island, too, looking out over a sandy nook to the water.

"When you can see the ocean every morning," he told them as they admired his view, "and the whales are right outside your window, it makes you feel like you're an integral part of it all. Just like your two families and the island."

While Hanna was glad that Joel had come to the interview with her as he'd promised, since he obviously didn't like the idea of her documentary, she'd been concerned that he might get in the way of the questions she needed to ask. Fortunately, though, so far Joel had simply greeted Milton warmly, asked him a couple of questions about the marine conservation boats, then let Hanna set up her camera and begin to ask questions without interruptions.

If anything, as the interview proceeded, Milton was the one making things a little tricky. Not deliberately, of course. It was just that keeping him focused on the events of 1951 meant continually drawing him away from all the stories he had of whale beach rescues and diving and the latest research from the scientists working with the local universities.

"Most of the researchers are all right," he said, sipping his coffee. Hanna had tasted hers, then politely put it to one side. Milton was obviously better with whales than coffee. "But you always get a few who think that because they've got a PhD, they know more than those of us who have been here on the island working with the sea for our entire lives."

"What about the Peterson–Walker wedding, Milton?" Hanna asked, gently steering things back on course. "Could you share some of your memories of that time with us?"

"I was just a little boy, but I can remember the preparations taking place all over the island. Everyone wanted to be a part of the wedding and the party that was planned for after, of course, but it wasn't all just about the big events. People on the island were genuinely happy for your families. The union seemed to make so much sense." He paused, looking back and forth between Hanna and Joel, ignoring the camera completely. "Although, now that I think about it, I'll bet this is one of the first times that a Peterson and a Walker have been under the same roof since then."

"We were at school together," Hanna pointed out.

"And there's the moment when Hanna came barging into my office yesterday," Joel added.

Milton waved their comments away. "Oh, those don't count. What I'm saying is that this has got to be the first time in more than six decades that members of your families have *willingly* been in the same room. I'll admit to being very surprised when Hanna let me know you would both be here today. Ever since Poppy's suicide, your two families have never been able to see eye to eye about anything, have they?"

An image of Joel's great aunt Poppy sailing off, despondent, into the ocean as a young woman leapt into Hanna's thoughts. But there were still so many things she didn't know that it was little more than a hazy image. For one, she didn't even have a good idea of what Poppy looked like. But before she could find out what she needed to know, she needed to make sure Joel would be okay with her questions.

"I'd like to ask Milton about Poppy, Joel. But only if you're okay with me doing so."

He seemed surprised by her question. And maybe even a little pleased that she'd thought to ask. "That's fine," he assured her.

The thing was, Hanna wasn't sure whether she believed him. Not when she'd seen for herself just how important the Peterson family history was to Joel, with Poppy's apparent suicide the most sensitive area of all.

This was her chance to—finally—get some answers. And yet, because she didn't want to hurt Joel, she found herself more than a little reluctant to ask, "Can you tell us what you remember about Poppy, Milton?"

"She disappeared a week after the wedding between William Walker II and Ava, and it was all anyone could talk about. Not only how both families were dealing with losing her, but also because everyone on the island was worried about losing their jobs."

Hanna tried to put herself in the shoes of the islanders in the early 1950s. A good filmmaker needed empathy; only, what was empathy but guesswork? Could she really ever know what it would have been like to have her livelihood caught between two families who had controlled most of the jobs on the island?

"There were all kinds of rumors flying around, too," Milton added.

"What rumors?"

From the uncomfortable look on Milton's face before he replied, she knew she probably wouldn't want to hear more. But that wasn't how documentary making worked. She had to film all of it, even if some of the things she learned were painful.

"As I said before, some of the rumors were about your family's berry business, of course," Milton explained. "Everyone thought your grandfather would sell, Hanna, but no one knew then what kind of deal he'd make, and the fear of that was worse than the reality of it, I suspect. Maybe that's why—"

When he stopped speaking she prompted him to continue. "You don't have to be worried about anything you say. It won't hurt my feelings, I promise."

"Well," he finally continued, "they said so many cruel things about Ava."

Her heart was thudding in her chest as Joel said, "Hanna, I know you want to make this documentary, but maybe this isn't something you need to know."

But she knew precisely how great her grandmother was. Which meant that anything cruel would have been a lie.

And how could she fight a lie if she didn't know which ones had been told?

Taking a deep breath to steady herself, she asked, "What kinds of things did they say?"

Milton looked deeply uncomfortable as he told her, "Well, you know that she used to dance in a gentlemen's club, which is very different from the clubs that dancers perform in nowadays. Much more respectable, elegant sometimes, even. And yet, back then you can imagine the things people said about Ava when they all believed that she'd not only stolen away the Walkers' heir, but also thought she was the one forcing him to sell the business."

Hanna winced. It must have been so hard for her grandmother to know people were whispering about her behind her back. And yet, when Hanna had announced that she was going to make this documentary, Ava had been selfless enough to tell Hanna to follow the story, despite knowing it would likely bring back all the whispers and the horrible assumptions again. Guilt twinged in Hanna's chest. She was going to give her grandmother the biggest hug in the world tonight.

"What about Poppy?" Hanna asked. "What were people saying about her? How did they feel about her sudden disappearance?"

Milton sat with his hands wrapped around the warmth of his coffee mug while he thought about his answer. "Most of them couldn't understand why a man like your grandfather would want to give up on a chance to marry Poppy for..."

"For a dancer he'd only just met?" Hanna supplied when Milton didn't finish that thought.

He nodded apologetically. "You know I adore your grandmother, but I'm afraid that was exactly what people thought. Plus, I think everyone felt terribly sorry for Poppy. They thought being jilted by her fiancé would follow her through life like a stain on her permanent record. My father actually quit working as an advisor for the families because he didn't want to be caught up in the middle of it all."

Hanna could sense that Milton was about to go off on another tangent. She would want to interview him about his father's role later, but not when he was talking about something that was far too important to step away from.

"When you say that being jilted by my grandfather would 'follow her through life', are you saying that Poppy felt ashamed? Cheated? Or something else perhaps?"

Again, Milton took his time thinking about her questions before he answered. "Honestly, I think everyone felt those things on her behalf, if that makes sense? I was just a kid, but I remember how people were talking about the fact that a jilted bride should be more upset by it all."

"More upset? I thought she committed suicide?"

"I know that's what happened," he said with a regretful glance towards Joel, "but even now, I can't look back without it seeming *wrong*. Because despite your grandfather leaving her for your grandmother, Poppy looked happy to me."

"Are you sure?" Hanna had to ask him. "After what had happened, she had plenty of reasons to be upset."

"I know," Milton said, "but I also know what I saw. All the *other* Petersons were upset. Some of them were furious about the deal with the Walkers being off, and some of them were furious at William for breaking off his engagement with

Poppy, but Poppy herself didn't seem to be angry or upset at all. In fact, the morning William and Ava got married, I saw her down in the soda shop, buying candy. She bought me an extra gum drop."

"Maybe she was trying to put a brave face on it," Hanna suggested.

"That's what everyone said when they saw her: how brave she was being. Some of them came out with some nonsense about people who have decided to kill themselves seeming happier once their mind is made up. But even when people started talking about her suicide note, I just couldn't believe it."

"Are you really saying that you think her suicide note wasn't a suicide note?" Joel asked.

It was the first thing Joel had said for quite a while. Hanna looked over to him again, just to check that he was okay. When she decided he looked more curious than angry, she turned back to Milton, who was nodding.

"Poppy was always writing poetry, scribbling away in notebooks. She read one to me once, but I was too young to really understand how good it was," Milton said. "I never got to see the final poem she left behind, but I heard it recited from memory a few times. The Petersons tried to keep it to themselves, but enough people saw it. And there were always a few kids who thought that Poppy's last poem was kind of romantic."

"That still doesn't explain why you think there was something, well, happy about it," Hanna said, unwilling to let the point go.

"It was the tone of the poem, I suppose. It's a little difficult to explain unless you've heard it, and I've never been much good at remembering poetry. But it certainly didn't sound like something written by someone who had given up all hope about their life." Milton shook his head. "Of course, I was just a kid, so maybe I was wrong."

When she could see that he didn't feel comfortable discussing Poppy's poem anymore, Hanna moved the interview on to his father's work with the Petersons and the Walkers, and then on to the conservation work he was doing these days. She wasn't sure any of that would make it into the documentary, except maybe as background, but why not shoot the footage while she had the chance?

In any case, talking about it certainly seemed to make Milton happier than he had been talking about Poppy. Thankfully, Joel's expression had also relaxed a fair bit by the time they finally said goodbye to Milton and started the walk back towards the center of town.

Even so, it took a few minutes for Hanna to pluck up the courage to say, "I think you and I both really need to see Poppy's last poem."

CHAPTER SIX

"You do have it, don't you?" Hanna asked when Joel didn't immediately respond. "It hasn't been lost or destroyed, has it?"

"It's at my house," he assured her. "I read it when I was a kid because my family wanted me to understand what had happened. And I know it will help your documentary." He sounded almost sympathetic. "But even at the time, my family didn't want too many people to see the note."

"I was fair about the interview, wasn't I?"

They stared at each other for a long moment before he finally said, "Okay, I'll let you look at it. But only because I can guess that if I don't, you'll probably go around the island looking for anyone who remembers a line or two of it to try to piece it together."

Hanna couldn't quite manage to hold back her smile. Clearly, they'd already spent enough time together for Joel to figure out that she was doggedly determined. Meanwhile, she'd learned that he would do anything to protect his family. Just like her.

She was caught between needing to get things to come together quickly for her documentary...and wishing that she could draw out this discovery period simply for the chance to spend more time with Joel so that she could learn more things about him.

"Once you read it," he informed her, "you'll see that Milton must have things wrong. He was just a kid at the time."

Even if Joel didn't think reading the poem was going to do any good, she was excited about getting to see inside his inner sanctum, and not just because she might learn something more about his family for her documentary.

No, it was simply because she wanted to learn more about *him.*

"So," she asked as they walked close enough to each other through the crowds of summer tourists that they could have easily been holding hands, "you don't think that there's a chance that Poppy's disappearance was, maybe, just a tragic accident?"

"She was from a shipping family. My father taught me to sail almost as soon as I could walk. Pretty much every weekend, we were out on the water. It would have been the same for her. And she would have known about the weather patterns and how to deal with even an unexpected storm."

Joel seemed far more relaxed on the walk to his house than he'd been with Milton. A couple of times, he stopped to briefly chat when people greeted them. Much in the same way that people always said hello to her because she was a Walker, she now realized that Joel got just as much attention thanks to being a Peterson.

There was one awkward moment, though, which came as they passed one of the island's older inhabitants. The gray-haired woman was carrying an easel, obviously one of the artists who called the island home.

"Shame," she muttered as the two of them went past.

"What's that?" Hanna asked, not understanding.

The look the woman gave her was actually a little frightening in its intensity. "I wasn't talking to you, girl." She turned her narrowed gaze to Joel. "Don't you have any shame, walking around with a Walker? What would your father think? What would your grandfather think?"

Hanna flinched even as Joel frowned and shook his head. "You should get on with your painting, Greta."

The woman scowled at him, then walked off.

"Thank you," Hanna said softly.

"It's not a problem."

But it clearly was. A *big* one. "People still obviously have some pretty strong feelings about you and me being together, don't they?"

"Of course they do. Did you honestly think

they wouldn't?"

And yet he'd stood up for her. What did that mean? Hanna resolved to give it some more thought later. *After* they'd looked at Poppy's final poem.

The Peterson house was just far enough away from his office that he wasn't actually living above his business, but still near enough that it was only a very short walk for Joel to get to work every morning. His home was old but well cared for, carefully re-painted as the ocean air wore it down. Even from the outside, it was easy to see that it was a house that had had a lot of love put into it.

"You know," Hanna said in her best imitation of Milton as Joel led her inside, "this is only the *second* time a Peterson and a Walker have been under the same roof in sixty years."

Beyond elated to finally get a real smile out of Joel, her heart was jumping in her chest as she turned to study the prints and photographs of the ocean in his hall, along with a large map of the island and the surrounding water. The furniture had a functional, masculine feel to it, and while she couldn't see him spending hours on interior design, she *could* see him carefully choosing everything in his home.

"That's the *Sea Spray*," Joel said, when he found her admiring a scale model of a mussel boat that sat on a plinth at the base of the stairs. "It's the first new boat I had built when I inherited the business."

It was hard, in a way, to imagine Joel being in a position to order up a new boat like that when, in her mind, he'd simply been the school quarterback she'd had a crush on. It struck her, yet again, that running his family business and being responsible for so many island jobs was a tremendous amount for one person to have to do. Plus, it was increasingly obvious to her just how much he loved the water. Truthfully, she could barely imagine him working in the Peterson Shipping offices all day. On the deck of one of his boats, maybe, but not in that small, stuffy space with a tie tight around his neck.

"I've put most of my family's old things upstairs in the attic."

It wasn't much more than a crawl space reached by a rickety-looking ladder, so Joel went first, taking a flashlight with him. Hanna followed him, taking his hand gratefully when he offered it to help her up.

As his hand clasped around hers and he drew her into the attic so that she was standing right in front of him, Hanna couldn't have denied how attracted she was to Joel, even if she'd wanted to. All she could think was that if she dared to lean in to press a kiss to his lips, it would *definitely* be the first time a Walker and a Peterson had kissed in sixty years.

Given the way Joel's eyes held hers, she was almost sure he was thinking the very same thing. But before she could risk everything on a kiss, he abruptly said, "I think Poppy's notebooks are towards the back."

Was he really so oblivious to her, she wondered as she breathed out a disappointed sigh when he moved away from her?

But how could he be when she could have sworn that his eyes heated more and more every time they came close like that?

Just as she needed to know the answers about what had really happened between the Petersons and the Walkers, she needed to understand this, too. "Joel—"

"I think I have it." He reached into the depths of the box, coming up with an old, leather bound notebook. There was a sheet of paper folded inside it, sticking out of one end. "This is the note. There's more light downstairs to read it by."

Just like that, the intimate moment was gone as Joel led the way back down the ladder, helping Hanna before closing up the attic again carefully. They took the old notebook downstairs to a living room where the coffee table looked like it had been lifted from a captain's cabin.

With Joel's permission, Hanna took out her camera, carefully filming as he laid out the note on the coffee table, making sure that she got a good shot of it before she moved in to read it aloud.

Happiness out of broken promises
Tossed across my family's waves
Passing out of a sea spray life
Sailing off into the sunset

I'll set my own course this time
Fresh beginnings rising on the morning tide

"It's been so long since I last read this," Joel said. "I'd forgotten what it was like."

"It's beautiful, and not nearly as dark as I expected," Hanna pointed out, reading through it again. "That part about rising on the morning tide…"

Joel shook his head. "My parents always told me that was because she expected her body to be washed up now that her future and her pride had been taken from her."

Hanna carefully kept the camera pointed at him. "Yes, but do you think that *now*, having read it again?"

Joel looked up, saw the camera and frowned slightly. "I don't know. There are a lot of things here about leaving the island behind, but there are phrases that sound like they're about new starts, I suppose. That part about 'fresh beginnings' and even the way the poem begins with the word 'happiness.'"

Hanna nodded. "It almost seems as if she was looking forward to what was coming. Maybe she wasn't as depressed as everyone thought she was."

"Or maybe you're just reading her poem like that because it's how you *want* things to be for your documentary."

Hanna lowered the camera. "I wouldn't do that, Joel. I *won't* do that. What I will do, however, is follow this story wherever it leads and do my very best to let the facts speak for themselves."

"But the facts don't speak for themselves," Joel insisted. "It's the person making the story who does that. And if you are the one telling the story—"

"Then all I can do is try to tell it as honestly as possible. And I will. I'm just here to try to get all the details." She needed to know, "Now that we've just started to break ground and learn something about what happened to our families in 1951 that changed everything on the island, are you really going to try telling me to stop?"

"Would you stop even if I asked you?"

"I need to tell this story," she told him in a quiet voice. "Don't you want answers?"

"Maybe," Joel admitted. "Look, I'll admit now that you've started digging into things, I've got questions, too. But this...this is a big step."

Hanna thought about reminding him of their deal—if he was happy with her interview, then he'd give her access to the archives. But Joel wasn't the kind of man that she could force into this or anything else.

"Listen," she said, "it's obvious you need some time to think about this, and I need to get over to the dance studio to film the students' dance recital. Ava, Emily, Rachel and her daughter Charlotte will all be there too."

"I've always wondered," he said, "what it would have been like to have a family that size?"

"It's utter chaos." But Hanna smiled as she said it. "The very best kind of chaos."

CHAPTER SEVEN

That evening as Hanna filmed the recital in her family's dance school, she thought about how nice it was to be back again. With its sprung floors and mirrors that ran the length of each wall, every inch of the studio brought back memories. She'd spent so many hours there as a young girl with her grandmother and sisters that it felt almost as much like coming home as going back to the house had been.

As she stood at the side of the small stage, Hanna was amazed, as always, by how gracefully the girls moved together across the dance floor. Grams had taught them well. Or more likely, these days, Paige had taught them while Ava looked on benevolently and made the occasional gentle correction to a student's stance or posture. Paige had been practically running the dance school for years now, even if she insisted that Grams was in charge. She opened the doors most mornings, she taught most of the classes, and now she was the one sitting at a table in the corner, smiling up at grateful parents while she signed their children up for the next semester of classes.

Hanna had danced a little when she was that age, mostly because she'd wanted to copy her big sisters, but she was definitely better off being the one filming the performance rather than being in it. And sometimes, she thought, watching from the sidelines could be as important as being out there in the thick of things. Someone had to tell the story, and it was because of the footage Hanna was shooting that both the parents and the students would have memories of this lovely recital years from now.

Though the performance was over, Hanna still kept the camera rolling. The recital had been carefully honed perfection. Everything else was real life: children running around laughing and playing while their parents tried to keep them in line, dancers congratulating each other, boyfriends holding bouquets of flowers.

Hanna noted that her little niece Charlotte was enjoying herself far more in the aftermath of the recital than she had at any point during it as the five-year-old ran away with a tutu on her head while Hanna's sister Rachel chased after her. Meanwhile, Emily was lining up the ballerinas for a photograph, trying to arrange the girls carefully by height while they kept wriggling out of position.

Hanna was the only sister not busy trying to

corral would-be dancers or sign up new students, and she considered pitching in to help Paige or Emily or Rachel, but from what she could see, they seemed to have it all under control. Besides, she was still busy capturing the joyful chaos of it all on camera.

She'd wondered more than once if this would always be her role in things: to be the one watching life happen while the others lived it?

Or was it simply that she'd learned to stay out of these things just because she was the youngest Walker sister?

After all, how many times, growing up, had the others gone out of their way to look after her? Especially after their mom died. It had been less like having four older sisters than four mothers, albeit ones who occasionally gossiped with her about cute boys at school.

Hanna swung her camera around to find the other member of their family. Michael might not actually be a Walker, but he'd spent so much time at the house that it amounted to almost the same thing. He was a good looking big brother, constantly there to help, and occasionally to annoy her. Though these days he seemed to do both with Emily more than any of them.

Currently, he was putting a band-aid on the knee of one of the ballerinas, whose mother hovered over Michael, staring at the scratch closely when he looked in her direction, but straight at Michael the rest of the time.

"Thank you for doing this," the woman was

saying as Hanna moved a little closer. "Maybe I could thank you by having you over for dinner?"

Hanna wondered how many of the other single mothers in the crowd cursed themselves in that moment for not thinking of the same ploy. Maybe not as many as might have done so if Michael hadn't shaken his head then, politely declining the way he so often did.

Finally, at the center of it all, there was Ava, surrounded by the children she'd taught. The parents all wanted to speak with her as well regarding which class she thought would be best for their child in the next semester, and if she thought they were dancing to their full potential.

Hanna didn't realize Emily had moved beside her until her sister asked, "Did you get all the footage you needed of the recital?"

She nodded. "I should be able to edit it tonight or tomorrow, and then the studio will have a finished piece for everyone to take home."

"That's great," Emily said with a nod of approval. It reminded Hanna of the times when she'd done well at school, and Emily had always made sure to tell her how well she'd done. "They like having the photographs, but it's the performance that they'll really remember. We all really appreciate you taking the time to help today, Hanna."

As they watched Charlotte spin around in Rachel's arms, Hanna said, "Do you ever think that one day you'll have your own?"

Emily smiled at that. "I already have four to

look after, named Rachel, Paige, Morgan and Hanna. Keeping up with all of you is more than enough for the moment."

"Hey!" She'd forgotten what it could be like, being the youngest, sometimes. Deciding to get in her own little dig, she said, "You know, Michael's been getting a lot of attention from one of the mothers."

Emily shrugged and said, "Good for him," but for a moment or two, it looked like Emily might head off in Michael's direction.

Instead, she remained with Hanna, looking over to where Ava was still chatting with parents and children, very much the center of attention. Their grandmother would kiss a cheek here, deposit some praise there. One of the mothers was reminiscing about when she'd been a student there herself, and Ava remembered every detail.

She remembers so much about the past, *but she won't tell me any of it,* thought Hanna.

Grams had said that she'd made a promise, but to whom? And why say that it might be time for Hanna to tell the story of what had happened in 1951 between Ava, William II and Poppy, if she wasn't going to talk about it?

"Everybody loves Grams," Hanna said.

"But they didn't always," Emily reminded her. "Everyone's so happy now, but that's just because we've come a long way from the days when half the island wanted to drive Grams out."

Hanna should have guessed that her big sister wasn't going to leave the topic of her documentary alone. It wasn't just that Emily had never been the type to leave things unfinished. Emily was as fiercely protective of Ava as any of Hanna's sisters. But what annoyed Hanna slightly was that her sister seemed to think she didn't care about Grams just as much as the others. What if there was more to the story that no one knew about? And what if what she and Joel had learned about the past changed everything?

"There was a time," Emily said, "when the Petersons and their supporters would probably have gotten out their pitchforks and flaming torches if they thought they could get away with it. Can you imagine what it would have been like for her?"

Actually, Hanna could imagine it all too easily. If she'd been one of the island's residents back in 1951, and the island's golden boy had broken off his engagement to marry a dancer from the big city, hating Ava would have been the obvious choice. Particularly once her grandfather sold the company, because it would have looked like William Walker II's new wife had talked him into it so that she could get her hands on the money. It would have been too easy to forget the part where the majority of the money went into building the school. And when Poppy disappeared…

"It must have been awful back then," she admitted. "But I never heard anyone talking about Grams doing all these terrible things growing up. And none of you ever said anything to me, either, about how cruel people had been."

"That doesn't mean that we didn't talk about it," Emily said. "We just didn't do it in front of you."

"You didn't have to protect me," Hanna insisted hotly. "You *don't* always have to protect me."

Emily put an arm around her. "You're our little sister. Of course we were going to protect you. And now you need to think about protecting Grams. She might have told you that what you're doing is okay, but you know she would never deny you anything. You need to think about the difficult memories and feelings that your documentary will dredge up and what they will mean for her. Do you want people talking about her like that again?"

That was the thing with Emily. She always managed to be so...so *reasonable,* even when she was telling you precisely how you needed to live your life. And the truth was that so much of it *was* reasonable, even if her sisters had no business hiding things from her.

"I promise that I have been thinking about all of that," Hanna told her. And for the time being, at least, that seemed to be good enough for Emily, who walked away to help Michael.

Hanna went back to filming the aftermath of the recital, but this time she focused just on Ava. Her grandmother had found a place in the middle of Walker Island's small community, and her importance in everyone's lives was reflected on the adoring faces of all the people around her.

If Hanna truly believed that making this documentary would hurt her grandmother, then she'd give it up in an instant, switch to Emily's whale migration suggestion, and hope for the best. Yet Grams had as good as *told* her to go for it: "*Maybe once you do make your documentary, it will finally be time that this story was told.*"

And when Hanna thought about Poppy's final poem...well, so many things just didn't feel right. Besides, if she gave up the documentary, she might not see Joel again.

Could she really just walk away from everything?

Taking a deep breath, she worked to push away thoughts of her deadline for showing the documentary to her professor before the end of summer. Right now, it was far more important that she make the *right* choice, rather than a quick one.

And in the meantime, she reflected with a small smile as Charlotte started to perform a very creative dance of her own invention with the borrowed tutu still on her head, there were plenty of other wonderful things to film on the island.

CHAPTER EIGHT

After Hanna left, Joel had tried to put his thoughts about Poppy aside so that he could get back to work, but even after spending the afternoon bogged down by meetings and phone calls and emails in the office, he hadn't been able to stop thinking about what else he might find in the attic. He'd gone back up and found a box with more of Poppy's journals in it, and for the past several days whenever he could carve out free time he'd read through them.

So far, he'd been through three thick journals, a couple of smaller notebooks, and a stack of letters. Not all of it had been poetry. Poppy had included diary entries and sketches of the island, along with letters from people long dead, and scribbled random thoughts. Yet her poetry was at the heart of it all.

Strangely, though one of the notebooks was dated from just before the wedding, he couldn't find any joyful or excited poems about her upcoming marriage. In fact, he didn't find any mention of the engagement or wedding plans at all. He was sure he was missing something and that there must be another special volume he hadn't yet found. But even after another exhaustive search of the boxes in the attic, he didn't find any new journals or poems that Poppy had written.

Perhaps, he thought on Sunday, as he sat in his living room and re-read the entries from the month before the wedding was supposed to take place in 1951, if he showed the journal to Hanna, she would be able to find Poppy's joy over her wedding.

Why hadn't Hanna been back to demand access to the archives as per their earlier agreement? Several days had passed, but there hadn't been so much as a phone call from her. Had she lost interest in doing the documentary?

Or in him?

Joel pushed that crazy thought aside as he closed the journal, then got out his cell phone. "Hi Hanna, it's Joel. I'm just calling to check whether you still wanted to go to the archives. Give me a call back when you get a chance."

Several hours later, however, he still hadn't heard back from her. And with the tourist season heating up, it meant Joel was soon going to be impossibly in demand over the next few weeks dealing with all of his skippers and their boats. If he and Hanna didn't go through the island's historic archives very soon, he simply wouldn't have the time to do it later without damaging the family business.

Last week, he would have been more than happy for the whole documentary to be forgotten. And yet, hadn't he seen for himself during their interview with Milton that she truly didn't intend to hurt anyone by telling this story...but also that something wasn't quite right about the story he'd believed to be true for so long?

If anyone was going to look deeper into the Peterson–Walker rift, he was starting to think it *should* be Hanna.

Now, he thought as he tried her cell again and got her voice mail, if only she would answer her phone. Joel looked out his living room window at the increasingly gray sky as he dragged on a coat. It was going to storm soon, and as the clouds grew thicker and darker and the wind grew colder and harsher, he realized the weather matched his mood perfectly. Joel felt like he was only barely holding back a storm inside himself, both with regards to his family's tragic past, and also to Hanna.

He desired her more than he'd ever desired another woman.

But she could never be his. *Never.*

* * *

With the help of some locals who had noticed Hanna heading through town with her video camera, Joel eventually found her out on the northernmost tip of the island, where the bluffs of rock sticking out into the ocean were sometimes battered by the storms that never seemed to touch the rest of it. In good weather, however, the beach at their base was a great place to gather for a party or just to sit and watch the ever-changing ocean.

He parked his car at the top of the cliffs then trekked down one of the trails which passed the caves that had sheltered some of the island's earliest settlers.

She was down on the stony beach by the bluffs, her camera on a tripod and pointed at a gathering set of storm clouds. In slightly faded jeans, a denim long-sleeved shirt, dark boots and her hair tied back to keep it from getting tangled in the rising wind, she looked a hundred times more amazing than any woman in an evening gown ever had.

Back in the attic, it had been all he could do to keep from pulling her against him and kissing her. She'd obviously wanted him to; yet that had just meant he'd needed to be the responsible one. The one who remembered just what a bad idea it would be for a Peterson and Walker to kiss after all these years.

But it was hard to remember the importance of being responsible as he looked at her gazing out over the ocean, looking at a storm as though it was the most beautiful thing in the world.

It wasn't. *She* was.

Still, it was a stupid idea to even think of

doing anything about it. On par with having foolish dreams about skippering boats when he'd been raised by his father to run the office.

Hanna was a Walker. Forget all those Romeo-and-Juliet fantasies of making things work out between the two families. Or better yet, *remember* what happened once their families got involved, and just how badly things had ended for everyone.

History had already proved that Petersons and Walkers just didn't go together.

Her eyes widened with surprise when she realized he was coming down the path toward her. But soon, her surprise gave way to a wide, and extremely beautiful, smile.

"Joel, what are you doing all the way out here?"

"I was wondering why I hadn't heard from you again about getting into the archives. Do you still want to go look at them?"

"Of course I do." But she looked more than a little stunned as she said, "You really came all this way to take me into them? Why?"

It was such a direct question that Joel wasn't prepared for it. Heck, he hadn't been prepared for any of this. His attraction to Hanna. Her endless curiosity and questions. And the fact that the Peterson-Walker feud suddenly didn't seem so cut-and–dried anymore.

"Does it matter? I thought you'd be happy about it."

"I am. But I'd still like to know what

changed."

Joel tried to think of how to explain it. "I've been looking through some of my family's old papers in the attic, and I have...not doubts exactly, but questions. And from what I can see, you're good at getting answers, Hanna. Because you see things most people would miss."

"Thank you," she said with a radiant smile that made his heart beat just a little bit faster than it already was just being near to her out on the cliffs. "That's one of the nicest things anyone has ever said to me."

Yet again, he wanted to put his hands on her waist and pull her against him so that he could finally see if her mouth tasted as sweet as it looked. Instead, he forcefully pushed away the urge as he asked her, "So you're here filming storms? Has your documentary taken a new direction I didn't hear about?"

"I needed some space, and time, to think about everything. So when I heard that there was a storm system coming in, I thought I might try to catch some footage. You know how rare storms are on the island."

The moderate climate on the island not only made berry picking so successful, it also meant that Peterson Shipping could often send ships to sea on days when companies based on the mainland had to stay carefully in the harbor.

"I still want to go into the archives, Joel," she explained. "But I didn't want to rush you—or myself—into making any hasty decisions. Just tell me when you're ready and I'll drop whatever I'm doing to go with you."

"Now."

"Now?" Hanna looked at him oddly. "What's the rush?"

"Things are about to get really busy for me at the office, so if you want me to take you into the archives, today is our best shot."

"Okay," Hanna said as she gave the rapidly darkening sky out over the ocean a slightly wistful look, "I'll just need to pack up my camera and then we can go."

The first rain fell in the lightest of dustings while the wind picked up. But moments later it was pouring down in splattering globules—more of a solid wall of water than individual droplets. The wind leapt to a roar, pushing at them hard enough that it almost tore Hanna's camera from its stand.

"The caves!" Joel yelled over the wind as he grabbed her tripod and backpack.

As they ran together up the rocky path, Hanna began to laugh. The whole situation was so crazy—running in the rain with a Walker he couldn't stop wanting to kiss—that Joel couldn't help joining in. They didn't stop running until they reached the mouth of the cave, huddling back from the sudden onslaught of the elements. Already, Joel was close to being soaked. Hanna was worse off, though, the storm having plastered her clothes to her body. Joel swallowed hard, trying not to stare, and failing miserably.

She was just so incredibly beautiful. Especially when he couldn't picture any of the women he'd dated over the past decade running through a storm laughing the way she had.

"A group of us used to come here in high school," Joel said to try to distract himself from just how close the two of them were in the small cave. "We'd go down on the beach and light a fire, then come back to the cave later."

"Rachel was in your grade at school," Hanna said. "Did she go to those parties?"

"I used to see her here sometimes, but we made sure to keep to opposite sides of whatever was going on." Now that he put it like that, it sounded so childish, not talking to someone because of something their family had done two generations back. "How is Rachel? She has a daughter, doesn't she?"

"She's great," Hanna said with a warm smile. "My five-year-old niece Charlotte keeps her pretty busy. Did you ever notice Rachel when you were at school? Or think about asking her out?"

That question caught Joel by surprise. "No. I mean, it never occurred to me. She was a Walker."

"Well, you're a Peterson," Hanna countered with a smile, "and I had a crush on you when I was a little girl."

But she wasn't a little girl anymore. Not even close. And if she were anyone else, Joel would be closing the space between them in a heartbeat, pressing Hanna back against the cave wall while he kissed her.

Of course, just then, the rain stopped, and he realized just how close he'd come to doing something truly crazy. "We should get to the archives."

Hanna stared at him for a long moment, her blue eyes darker than usual, before she finally nodded. "Okay, but I'm frozen. How about we stop off at the café first for a hot drink?"

"I don't know," he said slowly. "Do you think the world can handle a Walker and a Peterson being under the same roof for a *third* time?" he asked, only half kidding. Especially when he didn't know how well *he* was going to handle it himself, given that he'd almost just given in to kissing her breathless.

But Hanna didn't laugh. Instead, she simply said, "Honestly, I'm not sure I care anymore what anyone else thinks." And then she headed out of the cave and up the path to his car.

* * *

A short while later, they were sitting in the café, Joel with a cup of coffee, Hanna licking the whipped cream off the top of a mug of hot chocolate with her fingertip.

Just as he'd predicted, they got plenty of strange looks from the locals as they walked in together. Half of them probably wouldn't have looked so shocked if aliens had walked in.

Yet aside from the stares, coffee with Hanna felt surprisingly natural. She was easy to talk to, for one thing. And to listen to, as everything seemed to set her off on a new tangent.

"How did you get into filmmaking?"

"You know how they have screenings at the old theater in town? My sisters used to take me to everything that played, especially the black and whites." Her expression softened as she talked about her childhood and her family. "What's your favorite movie?"

Joel shrugged. "I don't really have one. I've never watched a lot of movies."

Her eyebrows went up. "You're kidding, right?"

"I didn't have four older sisters taking me to see movies," Joel pointed out.

"But movies—" Hanna still sounded like she couldn't quite believe what he'd said. "—they're such an important form of storytelling."

"And storytelling is important to you, isn't it?" His family had always been more concerned with making sure that he stayed grounded in the real world and that he followed the "rules" of that world, but clearly, the Walkers had encouraged Hanna to dream.

"Of course it's important," Hanna insisted. "Not just to me, but to everyone. Stories are how we understand things. How we make sense of them. How we pass ideas on to other people. Without stories, we probably wouldn't know half of what we do." She studied him over the rim of her mug. "When was the last time you went to see a movie?"

"Last year, maybe?"

"In that case, maybe you and I should go sometime?"

Part of Joel wanted to accept her invitation right there and then. But there were the archives to think about, among other issues. Like the fact that her family had betrayed his and had been enemies ever since.

Pushing back his chair, he said, "If we don't get to the historical society soon, we won't be able to go at all."

The archives were in a small annex next to the island's library and they decided to leave his car and walk over from the cafe. But they were only halfway there when the sky split open with rain again, the wind even stronger than it had been before.

And wouldn't you know it, they were standing right in front of the movie theater when the storm came again, fierce enough that they'd be doubly soaked if they kept on walking. Hanna took hold of his hand, pulling him back in the direction of the theater.

"You see," she said, "even the weather wants you to see more movies."

"It's certainly determined to push the two of us into cover. But what about the archives?"

"Come on Joel," Hanna said. "It will be fun, and the archives will still be there when we're finished."

The theater was showing the classic Bogart and Bacall movie *The Big Sleep*. Apparently, though, film noir wasn't all that popular on the island, because there were only a couple of other people in the theater. It made the whole place seem bigger—just him and Hanna while the Raymond Chandler story played out in front of them.

The movie was okay, Joel decided, but more than half the time, he found himself watching Hanna rather than the screen, unable to look away when her lips moved in synch with some of the lines of dialogue.

"There's a lot of symbolism in this next part," Hanna whispered at one point. "Not just the usual noir stuff of dark lighting to show the hidden darkness of the city, it's all about...sorry, I shouldn't be talking over the movie."

"No, that's fine," Joel whispered back.

Would she be surprised if she knew how much he was enjoying being with her, especially while she was utterly engrossed in something she loved so much? Enjoying it so much, in fact, that when the movie ended and the theater manager announced that an obscure Japanese monster movie would be screening next, and Hanna's face lit up, Joel almost decided to stay for a double feature.

He had never seriously considered the possibility of watching plastic monsters crush Tokyo—let alone alongside Hanna Walker—until that point. Yet he actually *did* consider it, at least until he looked at his watch and saw how late it was.

"Hanna, the archives."

"Yes, you're right," Hanna said. "I guess we'll just have to catch it another time."

Another time. Joel actually found himself smiling at that thought as they made their way out of the theater and back down the street to the archives.

He had a key, and let them both in. Inside, there were rows and rows of shelves holding hundreds of boxes. Benjamin and the others from the historical society did their best with the cataloguing and interpretation, but plenty of the documents there still weren't in any real order.

"This is amazing," Hanna said, clearly marveling at the sheer volume of files.

"If you'll let me know where you'd like to begin, hopefully it won't take me too long to find what you're looking for. Despite how disorganized it looks, there's actually some rhyme and reason to it all."

"More perfect chaos," she said with a smile, and then, "Why don't we start with the police reports of Poppy's death, along with the papers for the business sale."

He was pleased by how quickly he was able to find the reports. Hanna made some notes on the buyout, but the police report was what she really stared at for a long while.

"Is there a Coast Guard's report on Poppy's missing boat?"

Joel looked for one, and found it after a couple of minutes of searching. It didn't say much.

"They didn't find her body," Hanna said, her

camera still trained on the reports, just as it had been since they'd begun to comb through the historic documents. "And they never found any sign of the boat, either."

"It's a big ocean," Joel pointed out.

"It is." But Hanna didn't sound convinced. "But Poppy's poem...do *you* think it was a suicide note? Milton says she was too happy, and the poem talks about new starts, not death. What if we have this all wrong? What if *everyone* has it wrong?" She paused then, looking deeply concerned, as if she didn't want to have to ask the question they were both clearly thinking.

Their eyes were locked on one another's as he spoke them aloud. "What if she isn't dead?"

CHAPTER NINE

"But that's just...you can't be right."

An hour later, sitting with her sister and grandmother on the living room couch, Emily was reacting to the idea that Poppy Peterson might not have passed away in 1951 pretty much the way Hanna had suspected she would. For her part, Ava was listening quietly from an armchair. At least she wasn't brushing it all away as nonsense.

It was just the three of them for the moment. Rachel had taken Charlotte to a sleepover, while Paige was teaching a late class at the studio. Before Hanna had gone away to college, this would have seemed far too quiet. It had actually been pretty tricky getting used to having her own place when she left for school.

"Seriously, Hanna," Emily said, "you can't just go around coming up with ideas like this to make your documentary more exciting. I mean, what if someone sues you?"

"Who would sue me?" Hanna asked, slightly amused for once by her sister's overprotectiveness. "I'm not libeling anyone. The idea that Poppy might be alive doesn't imply that anyone else has done anything wrong. Maybe just the opposite, in fact."

"What about Joel Peterson?" Emily suggested. "I bet he wasn't pleased when you started suggesting this about his great aunt."

"Actually," she told her sister, "Joel's the one who asked the question." But she'd already been thinking it.

"Given how emotional this all is for him, I think he's being really reasonable about everything." Then again, it wasn't always easy to figure out what Joel was feeling and thinking. Especially when it came to her. There were moments when it seemed obvious that he was attracted to her, yet even when they were completely alone in the attic, and then the cave, he hadn't done anything. She'd felt his eyes on her at the movie theater too, but again, he hadn't made a move.

"A Peterson being reasonable?" Emily said. "That would be a first."

"You don't know him," Hanna insisted.

"I know his family has held a grudge against us for sixty years. Does that sound reasonable to you?"

"You don't know all the facts," Hanna shot back.

"Neither do you."

"Girls." Ava didn't need more than one word to stop them. "What have I told you about fighting over this?"

"Sorry Grams," Emily said, "but Hanna, this sounds less and less like you're making a simple documentary. It seems that you're determined to dredge up everything you can with an investigation that no one wants. And now you've even started adding in parts that can't be true."

"Why can't it?"

"Poppy Peterson drowned," Emily insisted.

"There's no direct evidence of that. We know she took a boat out in a storm. We know she didn't come back. No one found her or the boat. Plus there are other inconsistencies." Like a suicide note that seemed far too hopeful to be written by someone who was planning to end her life.

"Don't you think that if there were inconsistencies, someone would have picked up on them at the time? If there had been any suspicion about it, don't you think people would have looked into it?"

"I only know that it doesn't look right, so *I'm* looking into this."

Emily stood up. "You're impossible sometimes, Hanna."

Her oldest sister walked out, going through to the kitchen. Hanna could hear her pulling a tin of flour out of the pantry to begin baking. It was what she always did when she was annoyed.

"I'll talk to her, honey," Ava promised. "Right now she can't see that this is the path you have to go down. But I do, and I'll find a way to get her to understand that."

"She thinks that I'm still a little girl who she can tell what to do." Hanna couldn't keep a trace of anger out of her voice.

Ava moved to sit next to her. "Your sister did a lot to look after all of you after your mother passed away. Do you think that she's going to stop caring just because you're all grown up? Emily just wants what she thinks is best for everyone."

"And then gets angry when she doesn't get what she wants."

Ava shook her head sharply. "That's not Emily being angry, Hanna. She's just worried, that's all. Maybe she's even right to be, a little."

Hanna looked straight into her grandmother's warm eyes. "Are you saying I shouldn't do this?"

Ava smiled. "We've had that conversation. You know I think you should follow your dreams, no matter what. Now, I'm going to go talk to your sister."

"This would be a lot easier if you'd talk to *me*, Grams, by telling me what really happened."

Ava put a hand over hers. "We've had *that* conversation, too. You know I can't do that, sweetheart. You wouldn't want me breaking my promises, now would you?"

Hanna could remember when she was a little

girl how she'd been able to say anything to Ava, secure in the knowledge that she wouldn't tell anyone else. When her grandmother promised something, she kept that promise. No matter what. Grams wouldn't be Grams if she went around telling secrets.

"No, I wouldn't."

Her grandmother gave her a kiss on the forehead before she headed into the kitchen, just as the front door opened and Paige and Rachel walked in, both looking tired: Paige from her dance class, and Rachel...well, she seemed tired and stressed out pretty often.

"Emily's baking, huh?" Paige said as she looked through to the kitchen. She was dressed in tights and a leotard, the way she so often seemed to be. On the rare occasions she dressed up to perform, it came as a shock even to Hanna just how beautiful her sister could be. "Which means the two of you have been fighting, haven't you. Is it about your documentary again?"

That was the thing with having so many sisters. The odds on keeping anything a secret for more than a few minutes were pretty much nonexistent.

"I just said that I think there's a chance Poppy Peterson might not have died and she freaked out."

"Well," Rachel chipped in as she sat down on one side of Hanna and Paige sat on the other, "saying that Poppy might not be dead *is* a pretty big bomb to drop on everyone."

Rachel was the next eldest after Emily, and had always been gorgeous; yet these days she didn't seem to have the confidence that should have come with her position in the family and her looks. Even the way she dressed, in plain clothes that wouldn't matter when little Charlotte made a mess of them, seemed designed to avert attention.

"I know it is, but even Joel didn't react half as badly to the idea as Emily did."

"Joel Peterson?" Paige asked.

"And it's just 'Joel' now?" Rachel said. She and Paige glanced at one another. Hanna could guess a lot about that look, or maybe it was just the way *she* was feeling about him that made her feel they could see right through her.

"There's nothing going on between us."

"But that's not for want of you wishing there was, right?" Paige guessed with a smile.

Hanna could feel herself starting to blush, and that was just as telling as anything she could have said.

"We're not blind, you know," Paige said. "We can see the way you look every time you mention him."

"She's had a crush on him since school," Rachel added. "Used to follow him around everywhere."

"I'm *right here*, you know." She thought about standing up and walking out, but not only would that have been childish, it also wouldn't stop the others from just following her. Anyway, it was almost a relief to be able to talk about Joel.

"Is this just an extension of the crush you had on him when you were younger?" Paige asked. "I mean, he's quite a few years older than you."

"Seven years isn't that big of an age difference," she protested, "and this isn't some schoolgirl crush."

And yet, it was only as she said the words aloud that Hanna realized just how strong her feelings for Joel were growing.

"Plus, he's a Peterson," Rachel said.

"Who cares?" Hanna exclaimed, more frustrated than ever about the family feud that had taken over the island in the 50s and only seemed to grow in power with every decade that passed. "Do either of you actually think that there's something wrong with Joel just because he's a Peterson?"

"Well, no," Rachel admitted. Paige also shook her head.

"It seems to me like half the time, everyone is more concerned about what they think we *ought* to be feeling than with what we *do* feel." Hanna turned to Rachel. "Joel told me that when you had parties down near the bluffs, you'd keep to the opposite end of the party from him. Did you do that because you hated him?"

"No, but he was still a Peterson. I mean, it's just...*there*, isn't it? In any case, does he feel the same way about you?"

Hanna hesitated. "I don't know." She sighed. "Maybe."

"He hasn't said, or done, anything though?" Paige asked.

Hanna shook her head. She'd come back to the house tonight so excited after finally looking through the historical documents in the archives, yet now she felt on the verge of breaking into tears. Paige and Rachel seemed to sense that at the same time, because they both reached out to put an arm around her.

"Just because he's holding back now, doesn't mean he will hold back forever," Paige assured her. "You're amazing, Hanna. He's got to see that."

But Rachel, in typical Rachel style, took a different approach. "And if things go wrong, we'll be here for you."

Emily came back in then, but before Hanna could say anything, Paige let her know, "We've just been talking about Joel...and Hanna's feelings for him."

Emily simply stared at Hanna, before finally saying, "Couldn't you pick someone better to have a crush on?"

"It's not a crush!" Hanna insisted again. Just because she was the youngest didn't mean she didn't know what was inside her own mind and heart. "You don't know him, Emily. He doesn't have what we have together. He doesn't have a family to support him, to laugh with him, to cry with him. Can you imagine how lonely that would be?"

"There are days when I think it would be quieter," Emily said with a faint smile. "But yes, I can see that it would be hard to be all alone like he is. Still, though, I just don't see how it can work between you. Not with all of this family history, and all of these issues with Grams and what happened to his great aunt in the way." Emily paused and pinned Hanna with a very serious look. "Is this part of why you're so adamant about continuing to work on the documentary? So that you can be close to him?"

"Of course I want to be close to him," Hanna said, knowing there was no point in denying that now, "but even if he doesn't end up feeling the same way about me that I feel about him, I'd still need to finish my research and filming. Because I'm not the only one who needs to know what happened. Joel needs to know too, and I just want to give him the truth. I want to give *all* of us the truth, whatever it turns out to be."

"Come on, Emily," Paige said. "Lighten up a little."

"You can see how she feels about him," Rachel agreed.

Emily sighed, but sat down next to them all on the sofa. "I still think that this is a really bad idea. I don't want to see you get hurt. Any of you."

"Hadn't you noticed?" Rachel said. "We're all grown up now. We get to make mistakes and get hurt."

"And we also get to make seemingly crazy choices," Paige added, "like Hanna falling for Joel, that might end up being the right ones."

"Looks like I'm outvoted then," Emily said.

Hanna knew that no one but her actually got a vote on her love life. Still, it was nice to know that her sisters approved. Or, if they didn't exactly approve, they were at least willing to back her up.

Had Joel ever had that kind of support? Had he ever had anyone willing to go along with him even if they thought he was wrong, the way Emily was? Or to fight for his choices like Paige and Rachel had? Or to love him through right and wrong the way Grams did, no matter what?

"It's good to see you girls getting along again," Ava said from the doorway. "Does that mean that you've decided what you're doing next, Hanna?"

"I'm going forward with the documentary. And Grams, I know you won't talk to me about what happened, but do you have anything from that time? Joel's family kept all of Poppy's old notebooks, so maybe you have something like that?"

"You know what, I might have something. You'll have to look through quite a lot of my old things, though."

Ava led Hanna upstairs to her bedroom and opened her closet, revealing an old trunk at the bottom. "I suspect there will be one or two letters or photos in here that will interest you. Take it down to your sisters. I'm sure they'll want to help. I'm going to stay up here and head to bed. Goodnight, honey."

Hanna kissed her grandmother goodnight, then hauled out the trunk. It was heavier than it looked, but that was a good thing because it meant that there was more inside.

A lot more, as it turned out when she got it down to her sisters. Mementos from practically Ava's whole life. There were scrapbooks with clippings about the dance studio, photo albums filled with pictures of the five of them, and before that, pictures of their mother and father. There was even an old program from a club in Seattle, and a few letters that Hanna scanned one by one, looking for something relevant to Poppy's disappearance.

The others seemed to be enjoying the chance to go through Grams' old things just as much, but they didn't have the same sense of purpose as Hanna. Every so often, Paige would stop to comment on some of the dancers' costumes in an old picture from the school, or Rachel would ask a question about someone mentioned in a note. Emily, meanwhile, seemed satisfied with collecting the pictures of their mother.

Hanna finally found what she was looking for near the bottom, tucked away in an envelope. It was a single, unframed photograph, showing a much younger Ava standing with an arm around another woman's shoulders. Without the research she'd already done, Hanna wouldn't have recognized that second woman.

But now she knew Poppy Peterson immediately.

Still, she couldn't keep from saying aloud, "How can this even be *possible*?"

Why would Ava ever have her arm around Poppy? They should have hated one another. Poppy should have hated Ava at least. Yet there they were, both smiling. As far as she could tell, the picture wasn't taken anywhere on the island. Where could they have met?

Hanna stared at the photograph, looking for clues. There were buildings off to one side, on an angle, but it was the far background Hanna was looking at. The skyline had obviously changed a lot in the decades since, but she was *sure* that was the historic Times Square Building just visible in the corner. There might be no Space Needle or skyscrapers behind it, but this picture had definitely been taken in Seattle.

"Hanna?" Emily called after her when she immediately stood up and headed for the door. "Where are you going?"

"I have to tell Joel that I just found a picture of his great aunt and Grams together," Hanna explained, holding up the photograph. "And then...I think I'm going to need to go to Seattle in the morning to see if I can figure out exactly where they were."

"Seattle? Just like that you're leaving?" Emily threw up her hands in obvious surrender. "Okay, I'm not even going to argue. We both know you'll end up doing what you want, just like you always did when you were little."

Hanna turned around to give her big sister a hug. "I love you, you know. Even if you are the bossiest, most overbearing big sister in the world."

"I love you too," Emily said. "Even if you have always been the most troublemaking little sister in the world."

And as Hanna headed for the door, just for a moment she wondered if Emily had ever wished that she could run off to Seattle on a moment's notice, rather than taking care of the half-dozen things she probably had planned to take care of around the house and yard tomorrow? Somehow, though, Hanna doubted it. She and Emily had always had different dreams and goals for life.

But Emily was still the best sister Hanna could have asked for.

CHAPTER TEN

The morning ferry leaving the island wasn't particularly crowded as people were still more interested in getting onto the island than leaving it during whale season. There were a couple of teenage girls heading over to Seattle talking about a festival, a few islanders on shopping trips, and what looked like one of the marine biologists going to check back in with the university.

Plus Hanna and Joel.

They were headed to Seattle in the hope of finding out more about whatever time Poppy had spent there, armed with no more than a photograph and a lot of hope.

Joel was quiet beside her on the open deck, staring at the photograph. Hanna was slightly worried that the sea spray would damage it, yet, she didn't ask for it back, not when she knew Joel still wasn't entirely convinced that his great aunt could have been anywhere with Ava. After all, if two people should have hated one another, it was those two. The sheer incongruity of that photograph was likely what had brought him this far and had him taking a day off of work, when he'd previously told her how busy his schedule was becoming as the summer boating season ramped into overdrive.

Still, she couldn't help but hope that the photo—and the mystery it presented—wasn't the only reason he'd hopped on the ferry to Seattle with her. Because despite the boat not being overly crowded, Joel had chosen to sit right next to her. Close enough that she could feel the touch of his skin against hers when the roll of the boat pushed them together. A couple of times during the ride he'd looked over at her like he wanted to say something, but each time he turned back to the picture in silence.

She supposed she should have been surprised by how right it felt to be here with him, heading off to Seattle together to piece together Poppy's past. But as they sat beside each other on the ferry, she simply couldn't imagine taking this journey without him.

Every time she risked glancing at him, she caught him looking right back at her. The heat she'd seen in his eyes in the attic, in the cave, in the archives, was even hotter now...so hot that it almost made Hanna's skin burn.

"Don't you want to pull out your camera, Hanna?"

Her fingers fumbled a little as she reached for

it. "Good thinking." But even though it was a perfect summer day on the water, the sparkling blue water all around them couldn't hold a candle to Joel. "You look so right out here."

He smiled right into her lens. "I love being on the water. I always have."

Her video camera captured his wistful glance out across the Sound, and she suddenly found she had to swallow a lump in her throat as they headed into the city ferry terminal. If ever a man belonged on a boat rather than in an office, she thought, it was Joel.

A few minutes later when they'd arrived in Seattle, Joel leapt down onto the dock and extended a hand to help her down. Her foot caught slightly, so that for a moment she tottered there. She needed a hand free to catch her balance, but that would mean letting go of her camera. But she couldn't do that and lose everything she'd shot today.

Joel solved the problem by catching her around the waist and lifting her down to the dock. As he held her in the circle of his arms, she thought he actually might kiss her this time. But at the last moment he pulled back.

Just like he always had before.

"We need to hurry if we're going to find this place in the photo before it's time for the ferry back," he said.

He was right. Of course he was right. They only had a few hours before they needed to head back and she should be feeling excited about

Poppy and the documentary...not feeling sorry for herself because Joel didn't want to kiss her.

She took out the photograph, staring at it. "One house in the whole of Seattle—it might not even be there anymore."

"It's not the whole of the city, is it?" Joel pointed out, more positive than she was for once. "It's just like navigating a boat around the island. We simply need to look for landmarks."

Hanna nodded. She'd already identified the Times Square Building. So in theory, if they started there and set off in the right direction, she hoped they might actually be able to find it.

The ferry skipper interrupted that thought. "I hope everything's all right, Mr. Peterson? It isn't often you come aboard like this."

"Yes, Phil, everything's fine. I just needed to get to Seattle." Joel took the photograph from Hanna and showed it to the other man. "Do you know where this could be, apart from the Times Square Building? The picture was likely taken in the late forties or early fifties."

Phil shook his head. "Sorry, I'm afraid I don't. You really should talk to Frank as he's the only one who's been around long enough to remember the way the city used to look back then. He's piloting the ferry back this evening."

"Thanks for the suggestion, Phil." Joel turned back to Hanna. "Looks like we're going to have to do this the hard way."

"Spending the day with you in Seattle? It doesn't sound that hard to me," Hanna said before she could think not to.

Fortunately, Joel smiled back at her as he said, "We should get started."

What a long way we've come already, she thought, remembering the way he'd all but kicked her out of his office a week ago.

It was slow going in their taxi as the streets were full of hundreds of stalls and attractions set out in the sun for thousands of people to enjoy. Once they got to the Times Square Building they walked around it, taking in its square, heavily arched shape and the old architecture of the place, trying to work out the angle of it in the picture. Quickly realizing that the changes to the city since the 1950s would make following an orderly search through the city streets especially challenging, Joel bought a map of the city from the gift store, then took out a pen and drew a straight line out in the direction that they believed would get them to the location in the picture.

Heading out on foot, the area they were searching was right at the heart of the festival. Though Hanna knew they couldn't really afford the distractions, how could she resist pulling out her camera to film the colorful booths and displays and street dancers? And when her stomach started grumbling, Joel not only bought them both a spiced lamb kabob from a Moroccan food stand, he ended up eating half of hers as well. Almost as if, she found herself thinking, they were a real couple.

After four years at the university, Hanna was

always struck by how quickly Seattle transformed when a festival was in town. Each festival had its own character, and yet she suddenly realized that these seemingly strange and incongruous new elements were actually more like lenses and filters than completely different scenes—simply different ways of seeing the city to get through to the heart of it.

As they headed through the city, Hanna found herself thinking about Joel, and all the different facets of him that she'd discovered during the past few days.

He was a Peterson, the head of a long-owned family company, who needed to take charge of papers and meetings and phone calls, even while it seemed to her that the ocean was what really called to him.

He was the guy who'd been the star quarterback, the respected member of the island's small community, who was good looking and successful enough to have any woman he wanted, but was still unattached.

And he was also the man who hadn't been to a movie in years, who'd nearly kissed her half a dozen times by now...and who had actually been receptive to the shocking idea that his great aunt might not have taken her own life in 1951.

As much as Hanna knew that she should keep her camera on the festival or the surrounding neighborhood they were searching, it kept creeping back again and again to Joel.

"You love to look at everything through your

camera, don't you?"

"I don't want to miss the chance for great footage."

"But aren't you missing out on just experiencing some of it?"

"I think sometimes, I get to see more with the camera. People will open up to me in ways they never would otherwise." She gestured to a passing street performer, who was juggling flaming torches. "I get to see into the heart of things."

"Other people's hearts, maybe," Joel countered. "But what about yours?"

Her professor had said the same thing, yet coming from Joel, it felt like more. Hanna lowered the camera for a moment, looking at him. "What do you mean?"

"You're so interested in the rest of the world," Joel said, "but what about the things that are important to *you*?"

It was such a personal question that Hanna was momentarily stunned silent. "Doing this documentary on our families is important to me. And without it," she risked adding in a soft voice, "I would never have gotten to spend all this time with you."

Joel's eyes held her for a long moment before he finally said, "I get the feeling that you're going to be spending a lot more of today with me. You're right that looking for the location of this picture feels like trying to find a needle in a haystack."

And it was true. Finding one old house in a city the size of Seattle was seemingly impossible. Still, Joel didn't seem to mind looking with her as he asked her questions about landmarks like the Space Needle and the entrance to the Underground City. Unfortunately, though she'd spent four years at the University, for some reason she'd never made it a point to actually check these places out.

When she grew silent, he said, "Don't worry, Hanna, we'll just keep looking until we find it."

"No," she said with a small shake of her head. "That's not it. I mean, I know there's a good chance we won't strike gold today, but I'm dogged enough to keep looking even if we draw a blank this afternoon."

"Then why did you suddenly look so sad?"

Once again, he'd noticed her feelings. Even better, he'd asked her about them...almost as if he was really and truly beginning to care about her.

"I was just wondering, suddenly, why after four years at school here, I've never gone to the top of the Space Needle? Why did I stay in my little bubble and never really venture outside of it? Especially when I know I need to experience the world to be able to show it to other people through my films?"

"Well, since you took me to go see a movie at the old theater on the island, maybe I should take you to see the Space Needle now?"

Hanna thought he was joking, until a half-hour later when she found herself looking down at the city from way up high. "I'm pretty sure," she said in a voice that was full of emotion she couldn't manage to hide, "this is the first time a Peterson and a Walker have been to the top of the Space Needle together." As he laughed at what had become a special joke between them, she said, "Thank you for bringing me up here. Especially when I know we should still be down there looking for the house."

"Think of this as research," he said, although his eyes were warmer than she'd ever seen them. Almost as if he couldn't fight his feelings for her any longer, either. "We should work out where the landmarks are. Is that the Seahawks' stadium over there?"

Over the next half hour, they tried to pick out houses that looked like they might fit with the photograph, but from way up high, it was impossible. After heading back down, they passed a cluster of clubs with façades suggesting they went back a long way, but they were all so busy with paying tourists that no one had time to talk to Hanna and Joel about the old photographs. And since most of the staff were Hanna's age, she guessed that none of them would be that interested anyway.

Which was a problem, because it was starting to get late. They'd been walking around the city for hours now, and they still didn't have anything to go on.

"We're going to have to head back, aren't we?"

Joel nodded. "If we don't want to miss the ferry."

They took a taxi back to the docks where the ferry was waiting. Since they were at least a couple of minutes past the sailing time, Hanna guessed that the skipper knew his boss was coming. And when an older man, well weathered by the sea, with a beard that made him look like every caricature of a ship's captain Hanna had ever seen, met them out at the dock, how could she resist filming him?

"Mr. Peterson, there you are." The man raised a surprised eyebrow. "And Ms. Walker too. We were just getting ready to go."

"Thank you for waiting for us," Joel said, shaking his hand. "We won't keep you waiting any longer, Frank."

"Frank?" Hanna remembered what the skipper on the way there had said: that Frank had been doing this route long enough that he might remember the city back from the early 50s. It was a long shot, but after a day of looking, even long shots were worth trying. She put down her camera and took out the photograph of Ava and Poppy once more. "The skipper this morning said that you might know where this was taken. We've been looking for it most of the day."

Frank stared at it for a few seconds before nodding. "I believe it's from an old street of bed and breakfasts that artists used to stay in. I can give you the street on the way back if you like."

"Actually," Joel said, "it would be really

helpful if you could give us the address now."

"But if we go looking for it tonight," Hanna reminded Joel, "we won't be able to return to the island until tomorrow. And I know that you probably can't afford another day away from the office just to go running around Seattle with me."

"It's worth it to me," Joel said. "As long as staying in the city tonight is all right with you."

"Of course it is."

He took the address Frank had written down, then said, "Let's go find this B&B."

CHAPTER ELEVEN

Hanna held up the photograph, checking it against the house in front of her. The background had changed and it had clearly been repainted and repaired many times since Grams and Poppy stood in front of it, but the building was still undeniably the same, with a pre-war façade that stood out from the other buildings on the block.

"Wow, it's still here," Joel marveled. "I wasn't sure we'd find it."

He hadn't been sure, but he'd still come to Seattle with her—and now planned on spending the night there, too.

Amazing.

She held up her camera to record this moment and tried to think of something to say that would encapsulate how big their latest discovery was. But it looked like she was going to have to add the narration later, because right then her brain felt both too empty and too crowded all at the same time.

"Are you ready to go inside?"

"Are you?" she countered, in what might have been construed by someone who didn't know her very well as a playful tone, when the truth was that she was completely serious.

"I think we'd both be a little crazy to come all this way without going in."

Of course he wasn't going to back down. It was one of the things she liked so much about Joel. Just one of many.

Hanna swallowed hard as, camera in hand, they headed towards the bed and breakfast's door. Unfortunately, the woman at the reception counter inside didn't look like she was going to be able to provide much information on things that had happened in the fifties, because she wasn't much older than Hanna, though she dressed in a retro mid-century style.

"Hi there," the woman at the desk said. She didn't seem fazed by the camera, fortunately. "I'm Mandy."

"Hi Mandy." Hanna glanced around. It was like someone had taken everything they could find from 1900 through the 1950s and put it in one place, from whole rows of photographs on the walls to vases and furniture that fit the period. "This place is pretty...impressive."

"And hard to find," Joel added, stepping up beside her.

"We've been looking for it for most of the day."

"Well, you've made it here now." Mandy smiled. "What name is the reservation under?"

Hanna shook her head. "We don't have a reservation."

"You're in luck then. We were full up, but we've just had one room come available due to a last-minute cancellation."

Hanna moved the camera to explain. "We actually weren't planning to spend the night in the city, although now that the last ferry back to Walker Island has gone, I suppose we'll have to. Anyway," she added, "it's a little complicated, but I'm making a documentary about my family and Joel's family, and because we think they were here at some point, it would be really helpful if we could take a look around."

Mandy considered that for a moment and then nodded. "Sure. It's always nice to meet someone else with an enthusiasm for the past. Did you know that this bed and breakfast has been here for almost a hundred years now?"

"Well, we guessed it was here right around 1951," Hanna said. When exactly had Ava and Poppy been here? *Why* had they been here? Because if there were two people who definitely shouldn't have been here together, it was those two.

Of course, Hanna thought, there were plenty of people who would think that she and Joel shouldn't be there together, either. The question was, was Joel still one of them? Or had he begun to change his mind...

"This lamp came from an auction a couple of years back," Mandy told them, "and this desk is from my grandmother, who used to work here. This frame is from a private collector who I don't think really understood what they had, and..."

Hanna let the words wash over her. She should have been paying closer attention. She really should. After all, they'd finally run into the one person who seemed to know the history of this B&B better than anyone. Yet right then, all she could think about was Joel, watching him through her lens as he carefully picked up a small model sailboat to study it more closely.

"Hey! What are you doing?" a sharp voice said to Hanna's left.

She turned around, automatically bringing the camera with her to frame an older couple. She guessed they were there for the festival...but neither of them looked particularly happy.

"You can't just go around filming people like this in a public place," the man growled.

Mandy moved over to them, frowning. "Is there a problem, Mr. and Mrs. Smith?"

Hanna caught their slight pause at the generic surname Mandy had called them by and instantly guessed why a couple in a hotel wouldn't want to be caught on camera.

"You bet there's a problem," Mr. Smith insisted. "Do you always let people go around filming your guests like this? It's a gross invasion of privacy."

"She could be anyone," the woman with him

agreed.

Joel stepped up to them. "Like a private investigator, maybe?"

"What? No! Why would we—"

Joel held up a hand. "Hanna is a serious documentary maker. Do you think she'd be interested in *you*?"

A serious documentary maker.

Even her professors didn't describe her quite that way. Not yet, at least. Hearing it from Joel...well, Hanna couldn't think of anyone who had ever made her feel so good just by saying a few simple words.

"Even so," the man said, "she can't just go waving a video camera around. Who knows who might see the footage?"

Hanna was about to promise them that she would delete any footage with the two of them in it, but it seemed that Joel wasn't done defending her.

"Hanna would never do anything to hurt anyone. Don't you dare imply that she would."

As the couple stalked off in the direction of the rooms, Mandy moved to Hanna's side.

"I like your boyfriend's heroic streak."

"He's not..." Hanna began, but let it tail off. It would take too long to explain. Besides, with everything Joel had done for her—and the way her heart was pounding with gratitude and emotion for him in her chest right then—it was extremely hard not to wish that he was. "I won't use that footage."

"Since they don't have anything to do with what you're looking for," Mandy said, "I can't imagine you would." A bell rang from the dining room and she said, "We're going to begin serving dinner soon. Since you've found yourself unexpectedly staying over in Seattle for the night, are you sure you don't want to take my open room? With the festival, every other hotel I know of that's closer to the ferry terminal is fully booked, so you're lucky it's open. And I'll give you a good price too, since it's at the last minute."

Lucky. That was one way of putting it, considering Joel was probably freaking out at the idea of sharing a room with her, and being tempted to finally crash through the Peterson – Walker barrier that had been there for so many decades.

"We'll take it."

Hanna turned to Joel in surprise. "We will?"

"I think it would be best if we did, don't you, Hanna?"

The heat that had been in his eyes all day was burning hotter than ever as she agreed, "Yes, I do."

Their room was decorated in the same style as the rest of the hotel. The dresser was an antique, the closet was a heavily decorated affair with a mirrored front, and the mantel over the fireplace was elaborately carved.

And there was only one bed, of course. One very romantic looking bed.

"After you both get settled in, feel free to

come back down to explore more of the hotel's history and have some dinner."

Hanna nodded mutely. Already, she knew that after more than a few minutes in the same room as Joel she was going to have to get away. Because if she didn't...

"We'll be down soon," she promised, and Mandy pulled the door shut.

Just that simple act ratcheted up the tension in the room instantly. And now that they were alone, it was impossible to ignore how good Joel looked. How sweet he'd been all day.

And how badly she wanted to kiss him.

How would they manage to get through an entire night sharing a room?

"I can sleep on the floor," Joel suggested, in answer to her unspoken question.

"Don't be silly. There's lots of room for you on the bed. You could fit an army on that bed."

But in that moment as Joel's gaze locked with hers, it was obvious how much he wanted her. As much as she wanted him.

"It's not an army I'm worried about, Hanna." He looked slightly pained as he said, "I'm going to go splash some cold water on my face."

As he headed through to the bathroom, Hanna tried to distract herself, setting up her camera for a video diary of the day so far. Something for the documentary. Only, when it came to it, she didn't have the words. Not when all she could think about was Joel.

Turning off her camera, she took out her

phone and left a text message for her sisters. *Missed the ferry. Staying over in Seattle. I'm with Joel, so everything's fine.*

'Fine' didn't come close to covering it, but she knew better than to mention anything about sharing a room with Joel to her sisters. At this point, even mentioning him was a risk.

Hanna worked to clear her mind as she lay back on the bed, staring up at the ceiling. It wasn't like she'd brought an overnight bag, and she wasn't about to start taking anything off around Joel. Well...not unless he wanted her to.

No. It wasn't going to happen. *They* weren't going to happen.

When Joel came out of the bathroom, he stopped several feet from the bed, clearly afraid to get too close even though they were both fully clothed.

Hanna knew she needed to leave the room, and she needed to leave it quickly. Before she did or said something that he might not be able to forgive her for.

And maybe she would have actually managed it, had Joel not reached for her hand as she got up from the bed to pull her closer.

"Hanna?" His deep voice resonated all the way down to her toes. "I've been trying to fight this all week, but—"

With his hand over hers and his heated gaze warming her from the inside out, she couldn't stop herself from moving even closer, and whispering, "—now it's time for one more thing that a Peterson and a Walker haven't done together in sixty years, isn't it?"

And then she kissed him.

And, oh, the way he kissed her back made her breathless. His mouth on hers was hard and desperate one moment, then gentle and sweet the next. She tried to memorize every contour of his lips, the delicious roughness of his stubble against her cheek.

"I don't want you to sleep on the floor, and I don't want to just sleep," she said softly. "I know you think you're doing the right thing pulling back all the time, but you're not. I don't want to hold back with you anymore. Especially after getting to know you better and spending such a wonderful day with you. For one night, can't we just be who we are and feel how we feel without worrying about what happened between our families so many years ago?"

He didn't say *yes,* but he didn't need to, because the way he pulled her fiercely against him and claimed her mouth again was the only answer she needed.

And with Joel, she felt so safe, so perfect, that the moment was everything she could have ever wanted it to be.

CHAPTER TWELVE

The next morning, Hanna woke up with a smile on her lips. Last night had been perfect.

Absolutely *perfect*.

She felt full of energy and couldn't wait to see what the day would bring. After giving Joel a quick "good morning" kiss, she grabbed her clothes and practically bounced across the room into the bathroom.

After the day—and the night—they'd spent together, she *should* have been exhausted. Yet, as she showered and got dressed, she knew exactly why she was so full of energy.

She loved Joel. Loved him completely. Loved him with everything she was.

She never would have gone to bed with him if she didn't.

Joel would need to get back to the island today, but before that she hoped they could carve out a little more time to catch up with Mandy and get that tour through the bed and breakfast's past that they'd never quite gotten around to the night before.

Maybe they would learn something more about Poppy's past, and maybe they wouldn't, but just the thought of Joel being there with her, holding her hand while they searched together, was enough to send a warm glow straight through the middle of Hanna's heart.

* * *

By the time Hanna emerged from the shower, dressed again and lovely as ever, Joel figured he should have been used to her beauty. Especially after the hours they'd spent together in each other's arms the night before. But he was just as stunned as ever, so much so that he almost couldn't get his brain to work right and his fingers fumbled on the final button of his shirt.

"Are you ready to head downstairs? Because," she said with a grin that was at once pretty and sensual, "I'd be more than happy to stay up here."

Having a heck of a time trying to silence the voices inside his head that kept warning him he was making a huge mistake with her—and that if his father and grandfather were still alive they would never forgive him for allowing himself to get close to a Walker—he finally managed to say, "After missing dinner last night, we should probably go down and eat some breakfast."

One of them had to be sensible about this,

didn't they? Especially after last night had been anything but.

He could easily see the disappointment race across her face, before she quickly pushed it away. "I'll just make sure my camera's all charged and then I'll be ready to go down."

Only Hanna would need her video camera to go get breakfast. Joel smiled at that, and in that moment he wanted her as much as ever. Just watching her sleep when he'd woken a short while before her, his heart had been doing small flips in his chest as she lay cradled in his arms. And when she'd kissed him good morning, it had felt so right. Even now, it was all he could do to keep from kissing her again.

But it was just that thought—of how much he wanted her—that made him nervous.

He wanted so much, so quickly. And with a Walker, of all people.

A Walker who made his heart beat faster every time he looked into her eyes.

"I loved waking up next to you," she said in a soft voice as she slipped a hand into his. "I can't wait to do it again."

They were just a few simple words, but ones that hinted at so much more. Not just the perfect way they'd come together last night as man and woman...but at the possibility of a life together.

Again, his chest clenched tight at the thought of what his father and grandfather would think if they were still here to see him with Hanna. They'd be angry. So angry that he'd broken ranks and had let himself fall for her.

Downstairs, Mandy was already serving up breakfast to several other guests. Thanks to Hanna and her friendly questions, Joel soon found out that the gray haired couple had been to the festival every year for a couple of decades now, the group of college students had come from Vancouver to enjoy the big event for the first time, and the two women sitting together had come all the way from New York.

"What do you do when you're not traveling to festivals?" she asked one of the women.

"I work in pyrotechnics."

"Like firework displays?"

"Mostly movies and TV shows, actually."

"Wow, so maybe the next time my sister Morgan does the makeup for a movie action sequence, there's a chance you'll be there, too?"

"Your sister works in movies?"

Soon everyone was chatting together, the conversation moving easily from movie sets to artists' studios in Seattle to everyone's stories about the festival. Joel could have joined in. Instead, he sat back, watching Hanna at work. This side of her, the side that went out and tried to learn all about people's lives, was just as beautiful as all the others. She got answers from people because she genuinely seemed to want to know about them. She genuinely cared.

"Are all of you studying anthropology?" Hanna said to the group of college students who had come in from Vancouver for the festival. "I know I might be biased, but I think that you would find a trip to Walker Island really amazing for your studies. And just to have fun, too."

Always the island. Joel couldn't blame Hanna for how everything came back around to it—not when his own life revolved around it, too. And not when he loved Walker Island just as much as she did.

Yet that was the problem right there. It was *Walker* Island. Every mention of it inevitably came with a reminder that they weren't just two people who were falling for each other. On the contrary, they each came with deep family histories full of heartache and betrayal. But for a little while, at least, he'd been able to forget the past, and concentrate, instead, on the way that Hanna seemed to give other people's lives more meaning just by paying attention to them.

Just the way she has with mine.

Hanna reached over to touch his hand. "We should probably find Mandy. I want to see if she can tell us anything before we go."

When they found the B&B's manager in the kitchen, she asked, "How was your evening?"

"The room was lovely and the bed was very comfortable."

Joel thought Hanna was blushing a little as she said it, but not enough that anyone who didn't know her well would notice.

"We were hoping that you might know someone who remembers this place from the fifties that we could speak to?"

"My grandmother used to run the hotel, but now it's just me. But I know pretty much everything there is to know about the history of the place."

Hanna took out the photograph of Poppy and Ava, pointing at Poppy. "I'm trying to find out more about this woman. We were wondering, if you have any old account books or journals, perhaps we could find out if she was a guest here."

"Why are you looking for her?" Mandy asked. "Who is she?"

"Her name is Poppy." Hanna looked across to Joel, a question in her eyes. When he nodded that it was okay to say more, she said, "Poppy Peterson. She was Joel's great aunt and the woman in the picture with her is my grandmother. We think this picture probably dates back to the late forties or early fifties. She's been, well, missing for a very long time, and we're trying to figure out what really happened to her."

Now Mandy looked sympathetic. "I'm happy to help if I can. Just give me a minute."

She went off into the back room and when she came back, she said, "These are the working ledgers from around that time. They're like a big diary of the old place."

The stack of ledgers was huge and Joel had to admit that, all along, he'd known there was only a limited chance of finding any reference to his Great Aunt Poppy here. And yet, he'd still taken two days off from Peterson Shipping during the busiest season of the year to dash across to Seattle with Hanna.

It was madness, looked at that way...madness that only worked if he didn't allow himself to look too hard at it.

"I think I have something!" Hanna declared after only a few minutes of reading. "Joel, you'll be able to tell better than I can."

Surprised that she could have found anything so quickly, he read through a couple of housekeeping notes on the need for more towels and a request for an afternoon off that didn't seem like anything special, even though it was signed 'P.'

But then, he took a closer look at the handwriting.

"Do you see how similar her handwriting looks to the poem?"

Joel could see it easily enough, but he was too shocked to believe it was true.

The date was 1952. A year after Poppy was supposed to have passed away.

"Do you know who could have written this note?" Hanna asked Mandy.

"If I'm remembering what my grandmother told me correctly, that would be one of the chamber maids. Penny, I think she was called when they noted her wages." Mandy flicked through the book, and sure enough, there was a wage sheet showing half a dozen people, one of them listed simply as Penny P. "Let's see, she worked here for about a year before leaving."

Hanna asked Mandy for more details, but Joel needed some air, so he slipped out of the room and went to stand on the front porch. As much as he wanted to deny it, the handwriting was definitely the same.

Which meant that his great aunt hadn't died when everyone thought she had.

Instead...she'd run off to become a chambermaid in a bed and breakfast in Seattle.

"Joel?" Hanna stepped out on the porch beside him. "Are you okay? Aren't you happy that we know for sure now that Poppy didn't commit suicide?"

"It means she left, Hanna." His voice sounded hollow even to his own ears. "It means she abandoned her family."

Poppy had abandoned everyone around her. Just left. The way everyone in his family seemed to.

Joel's parents and grandparents had died years ago. His aunt, uncle and cousins who lived off the island had disappeared as soon as they were able, leaving him with the company to run, regardless of whether it was what he wanted, and only very rarely visited.

And now he'd just found out that his family's most tragic figure had been just as selfish as the rest of them?

"Even so—" Hanna began, reaching out for him, but Joel stepped away from her.

He could see the hurt register on her face as he did so, but he hurt too much himself right then to stop himself from pulling away.

Pulling away completely.

"This was a mistake. All of it. Allowing you into the archives. Looking into Poppy's past. Coming here to Seattle to hunt down a house in an old picture."

"What about last night? Do you think that was a mistake, too?"

Joel had wanted to allow the beauty of being with Hanna to override common sense. But now he knew for sure that if Poppy could just leave the way she did, without giving so much as a thought to the people who loved her, then *anyone* could leave.

"Yes, it was a mistake. One I tried so hard not to make with you."

He knew how much his words had to hurt her, but she didn't cry. Didn't run.

She did the exact opposite in fact, saying, "I know it wasn't a mistake. Nothing that beautiful could be."

Her absolute certainty that they were good together regardless of what anyone thought shook him to his very core. "When you told me you were going to make this documentary," he reminded her, "you told me flat out that it was so that you could get into the graduate program. And when you do, you're going to leave."

The way everyone left. The way his parents had. The way his aunts and uncles and cousins had.

The way Poppy had.

"But I lo—"

Joel cut Hanna off before she could finish. "And even if you did stay...if you stayed because of me...that would be just as bad, because then I'd be the guy forcing you to give up your dream. It wouldn't be right. Not for either of us."

He knew the right thing to do now. Had known it all along, actually, but had been so tempted by Hanna's smiles, by her laughter, by her beautiful blue eyes that so captivated him, by her intelligence and passion, that he'd ignored common sense.

"You should get going if you aren't going to miss the ferry back to the island, Hanna. I'll get a ride back on one of the mussel boats."

He let himself look at her one last time, let himself remember how good it had been to be with her, before he made sure he was the one walking away this time.

CHAPTER THIRTEEN

Hanna wasn't entirely sure how she got home. She could barely remember making her way back through Seattle, the festival still going on all around her. It had seemed so wrong that the rest of the world could still be enjoying itself when Joel had just broken her heart. Shattered it into a million pieces, actually. And she barely remembered the ferry ride, either, wondering the whole time how Joel could walk away from her without a second glance.

Finally back at the Walker house, she stumbled in through the door. When Charlotte hollered, "Aunt Hanna is back home!" she gave her niece a quick hug before quickly heading upstairs so that Charlotte wouldn't see the tears she was only just starting to let fall.

A short while later, Emily opened up her bedroom door, and as she sat beside Hanna, her oldest sister put an arm around her. "We got your message," Emily said gently. "What happened?"

"Joel and I..."

Hanna shook her head. She could easily imagine everything Emily was going to say about her sleeping with Joel. *How could she be so stupid, starting something with a Peterson? And, couldn't she see that he was completely wrong for her?*

But that was the problem. Hanna couldn't see that. She loved him. She loved him, and he'd walked away as if what they'd shared together had been nothing.

As if *she* was nothing.

"We guessed that part," Emily said softly, but instead of lecturing her or saying *I told you so*, Emily simply drew Hanna closer. "I thought being with Joel would make you happy, Hanna."

"I was happy. So happy, Emily. Until he walked away."

"Then you deserve better than him."

But that was just the problem, Hanna thought as she wiped away her tears, there *wasn't* better than Joel, and now he was gone. He was gone, and the simple fact of that felt like a black hole opening up inside her, devouring everything else.

But Hanna knew Emily wouldn't understand, especially not when all she could see was that Joel Peterson had made her youngest sister cry. A part of her wanted so badly to confide all of her hopes, her fears, her dreams to her sister, but another part just wanted to be alone.

Eventually when she stayed quiet, Emily left, saying something about going downstairs to fix something for Hanna to eat. Was it lunch or dinner? Hanna wasn't sure. She didn't even know how long she'd been there anymore. She wasn't hungry, in any case.

A few minutes after Emily left, Rachel came in. Her second eldest sister took her hand. "I know it hurts when a guy just walks out on you," she said, obviously having already spoken with Emily.

Hanna could see the pain still there in her sister's eyes from when Charlotte's father had walked out on Rachel. Not only did she have to cope on her own as a single mother every day, but she'd also shut herself away from other romantic relationships so that she wouldn't be hurt again.

"Joel didn't just walk out on me, at least not right away. We found out some things about Poppy in Seattle first. Important things."

"But after you did, he didn't want you messing with his family anymore, did he?" Rachel guessed.

"No, he wasn't angry with me for pursuing my documentary anymore, not when he'd agreed to join me in the search for information. It was what he found out about Poppy that made him angry. She didn't end her life after her engagement fell apart; she moved on to a new life in Seattle instead, without telling anyone in her family." Hanna was still trying to make sense of it all. "He was angry, so angry, when he found out that she'd walked away from her family without a second thought. And then *he* walked out on *me* the same way."

Rachel squeezed her hand. "I'm pretty sure that if men made sense, the whole world would be a simpler place. But you have us, and we'll make sure you don't need to worry about him anymore."

It wasn't that simple though. Hanna couldn't just put Joel behind her and move on with her life.

Not when she still loved him.

And not when she could still remember the pain in Joel's voice as he'd told her that he couldn't see her anymore. He'd seemed so certain that she was going to leave him, just like Poppy had left her family behind all those years ago.

"One day," Rachel promised, "it will hurt less and everything will pretty much go back to normal."

But Hanna didn't want her old normal. She wanted Joel, wanted the fantasy of a life with him that she could so easily see, and feel deep inside her heart, to be her *new* normal.

"Charlotte painted you a picture. Well, it's more of a handprint, really."

"That's so sweet of her." Hanna tried to force a smile, but she couldn't. She also didn't want her little niece seeing her like this, or to grow up believing that falling in love meant getting hurt. "I'm not sure—"

"I know. Whenever you're ready, I'll let her come up to say hello. Now, I should probably go check on her before she decides to repaint the walls with crayons."

A few minutes later, Paige popped her head in the door. "I guess you must be pretty sick of all of us coming to check that you're okay by now."

Hanna shook her head. "No, I would never get sick of any of you."

"I got a few details downstairs," Paige said as she sat down on the bed with her usual grace, "enough to guess that Emily played the big-sister-knowing-best card and Rachel probably told you all men are unpredictable pigs." Paige hugged her. "Which is why I thought I'd just sit here with you until you felt like kicking me out."

Hanna loved each of her sisters, but they'd always related to each other in different ways. Emily had been the one who had told Hanna how to solve her problems, Rachel had once been the slightly wild one who always seemed to have done everything first and had ended up broken from the risks she'd taken, and Paige, while older than Hanna, had never judged anyone's choices. She'd simply been there to listen, and to talk things through, if Hanna needed to.

"I slept with Joel in Seattle."

Paige kept sitting there, just listening, the way she'd promised she would.

"Then in the morning, after breakfast, he told me we'd made a mistake by being together. You're right that Emily and Rachel think he walked away from me because he's a Peterson, or because it's what men do."

"Why do you think he left?"

"We found out that Poppy had worked as a

chamber maid at the B&B we stayed at. In 1952."

"But," Paige said in clear surprise, "she died in 1951."

"No," Hanna confirmed, "she definitely didn't. And once we learned that she must have escaped the island, and her family, to live a new life, Joel started talking about how people always walk away...and how I was going to do the very same thing as soon as I'd finished the documentary."

Paige didn't say anything that time. She'd always been good at not saying things.

"And the truth is," Hanna said, "I don't *know* if I was going to. I mean, the graduate film program is what I've been working towards since pretty much forever. But I didn't know I was going to fall in love with Joel. Why couldn't he have let me have some time to think? To figure things out? Why did he just have to push me out of his life like that?"

Paige put both of her arms around Hanna. "We're all here for you. Whatever you need. You know that, right?"

Of course, that was right when Hanna's phone rang. Morgan was calling from New York.

Paige let herself out as Hanna picked up to speak with her sister, who immediately launched in with, "Emily and Rachel called to tell me about your documentary, and how you need it for your grad program acceptance...and also what happened with Joel walking away from you so that you wouldn't be able to leave him first. Are you okay?"

Hanna appreciated, more than she could ever tell her sister, that Morgan hadn't simply offered to make some calls to the film program on her behalf. "Thank you for calling to check in on me. It's so nice to hear your voice. But..." She couldn't lie and say she was okay. Not when she really, really wasn't just then.

"You're amazing, Hanna. Even when we were little kids you always had such vision, and such a knack for telling an engaging story. And you also have one of the biggest, most open and honest hearts of anyone I've ever met. I don't know Joel beyond seeing him at school and around town when we were kids, but I have to believe that way down deep in his heart he must know you would never leave him the way the rest of his family did." Hanna could hear someone talking to Morgan in the background. "I'm sorry," her sister said in a low voice, "but I need to go right now or the movie star I'm working with will have a major hissy fit."

Hanging up the phone, Hanna thought about what Morgan had said, particularly about Hanna's honesty.

She'd given him everything last night, yet the truth was she'd still been shooting for her place in the masters program. What, she had to ask herself, would have happened if she'd gotten it? Would she just have left Joel behind?

No. For as much as the program meant to her, she couldn't have just left him like that, and why would she when surely there was a compromise they could figure out so that they could be together while both pursuing their dreams.

What's more, Hanna simply couldn't believe that Poppy had abandoned her family like that either. Not unless Joel's great aunt hadn't had any other choice.

Yet that was what all the evidence seemed to point to, that Poppy had run off to Seattle and let everyone think Ava and William had driven her to suicide, the stigma of it following them around for years.

There was a soft knock on the door before her grandmother stepped inside. "Hanna, darling."

Of course Grams would be there for her when she was upset, the same way she'd been there for Hanna with every scraped knee and tear in her childhood.

Ava sat down on the bed next to Hanna, holding a small cardboard box. "Your sisters have told me quite a lot of what is going on." She brushed aside a strand of Hanna's hair. "Though I'm not quite sure that any of them got the whole story, did they? You do love Joel, don't you?"

Hanna nodded without hesitation.

"I'd like to tell you what I know of Poppy Peterson now, if you still want me to."

"I thought you made a promise?"

"I did. And I've kept it so long that it's almost a part of me now. Everyone involved is dead. Even so, I've done my best."

"Then why break it now?"

"Because it was a promise given to spare people pain, yet now you and Joel are both hurting deeply because of it. Poppy wouldn't have wanted that, Hanna. You'd have liked her if you'd known her. And I know she would have liked you, too." Ava opened up the box. It was full of old envelopes. "If you're wondering why you've never seen these before, it's because I kept these in a special place where curious little girls couldn't find them," she said with a small smile. Ava reached into one of the envelopes and pulled out a postcard. "William and I received the first one about a week after Poppy left. It just said 'I'm okay.' She didn't sign her name, but we immediately knew it was from her. She always sent them in envelopes where she typed our names and address on the outside, probably so that no one in the post office would recognize her handwriting on the actual postcards. And we never showed them to anyone else, but we kept them all."

"I don't understand," Hanna said as Ava passed her the envelopes and she pulled out postcards one after the other. The first ones were all clearly sent from Seattle, but the others were from different places, seemingly all around the country. "What happened back then, Grams?"

"The first thing you have to understand is that William and Poppy never loved one another. They loved their families, but their families loved their positions on the island as much as they loved their children. Or perhaps I just have harsher memories of that situation than most."

It was understandable that she would, given how people had treated her after she and William had married and Poppy had disappeared. Hanna didn't say that though. She just let her grandmother keep telling the story.

"Everybody said what a good match William and Poppy were. Even over in the city, where I was a dancer, the news was of how the marriage between the son of the berry magnates and the daughter of the ship owners would join together two powerful businesses. Always the businesses, mind you, and never a word about love. And when I met William, I knew at once that he didn't love Poppy. Which was just as well, because I loved him from the very start. It turned out that he loved me too, though he was extremely reluctant to hurt Poppy, because he actually thought she might love him. So we did the sensible thing and met with her in Seattle, on the pretense of a shopping trip, to ask her."

"She didn't love him?"

Ava smiled. "It turned out that she didn't love William any more than he did her. And she didn't care for the life that had been planned out for her by her family, either. She wanted to be a poet, wanted to be so much more than just a means of joining together two families. Just as your grandfather simply wanted to be a teacher, not a business magnate."

"So you plotted this between you?"

"Plotted is a strong word," Ava replied. "But

yes, we discussed it. We decided we would be happy. All of us. William and I would be married, presenting his family with a fait accompli, leaving Poppy free to pursue her dreams."

"But you let people believe she was dead," Hanna said, her voice rising as everything she'd been feeling came out. "You let them blame you for her suicide."

"Poppy gave me William. She left me the love of my life. The least I could do was help give her a chance at her dreams." Putting her hand over Hanna's, Ava explained, "You have to understand the way it was back then, the way it still often is now. If her family had known she was alive, do you think they would have let her go? The idea was that eventually, once she had made her new life, she would come back strong and able to face her family knowing they couldn't sway her or pressure her into following their rules, rather than her own." Ava looked back down at the postcards. "I met with her once or twice afterwards, before she left Seattle. After that, it was only postcards, and even those stopped after a couple of years."

Hanna sat there staring at the postcards. "What should I do, Grams?"

"That's for you to decide, darling. Well, you *could* go downstairs and let your sisters decide for you, but trust me, William and I were happier when we made our own choice. I'd like to think that ultimately, so was Poppy. I don't know for sure how things turned out for her after she stopped sending the postcards. All I know is what she wanted, what she dreamed of. Just the way you've always known what you want and have followed your own dreams."

With that, Ava pressed a kiss to her forehead, then left her alone with the box on her lap.

* * *

Joel guided the mussel boat back into the harbor slowly, piloting it with the skills he'd kept honed throughout his time as the Peterson Shipping Company's head. Unfortunately, however, it said a lot about how little time he'd been able to get out on the water in recent years when the captain had looked worried as he'd first taken the wheel.

"It might be the company's boat, sir, but I'd hate for anything to go wrong."

But Joel had deftly piloted the mussel boat, concentrating to keep it steady. The captain seemed bothered by the way the salt spray got onto his suit, but Joel was simply glad for the chance to pull off his jacket and toss his tie on top of it.

The crew dove for the mussels rather than dredging, just one of the many ways they tried to protect the ocean around the island. They loved the sea too much for anything else.

And they weren't the only ones who loved it. Joel did, too, from as far back as he could remember.

There was something so simple, so pure

about being on the water. Finally, after everything that had happened this week, he was able to think clearly...and, of course, all he thought about was Hanna.

Could he have done something else?

Could he have made a different choice?

Because if she was going to leave the island to pursue her dreams, then what future was there for them? Especially when he cared so much for her that he would never want to be the guy holding her back, trapping her on the island when she should be doing what she loved.

Which reminded him, while he was out here playing with boats, there was plenty of paperwork waiting for him back at the office.

"Anyone can be a captain," his father had often told him, *"But there's only one head of the company. Duty comes first, Joel."*

Duty.

Joel's sigh came almost at the same moment the mussel boat touched the dock. Everything in his life had been about duty. Duty and seeing things through.

Yet, hadn't he left one thing unfinished?

One very, very important thing.

The captain of the mussel boat shook Joel's hand as he hopped down onto the dock. "I'm glad you could come out with us today, Mr. Peterson."

"Joel, please. Just Joel, not Mr. Peterson."

"Well, Joel, if you ever feel like coming out again, I'd be glad to have you." The gray haired man gave him an unexpectedly empathetic look.

"And I hope that whatever you were thinking about, that the sea helped you find an answer."

CHAPTER FOURTEEN

After Ava left, Hanna stared at the postcards for a long time, more evidence that Poppy had left her family behind.

Hanna suddenly pushed the postcards and envelopes away. Everything she'd touched with this documentary was too close, too personal. If it wasn't hurting Joel by digging up the past, it was upsetting her sisters or making Grams break her promises.

"Show me your heart...that's the difference between a real documentary maker and everyone else."

It hadn't sounded easy—she'd known better than to assume that it would be—but at the same time, hadn't she assumed that everything would work out for her the way it always had? She'd barged into the Peterson Shipping offices because she needed access to the archives so that she could make a good enough documentary to get into the master's program. She'd made Joel show her his aunt's poems and the police reports because she needed to follow Poppy's trail no matter whom it hurt. And she'd pulled him onto a ferry to Seattle with her because she needed to show him that everyone was wrong about what had happened in 1951.

Thinking back on her childhood, Hanna couldn't remember a time when she hadn't gotten what she wanted. With four big sisters, not to mention the famous Walker name to fall back on, she'd always had things easy. When she'd fallen as a child, Grams had always been there to pick her up. Emily had helped her with her homework, even making it seem like fun. Rachel had taken her to parties, never complaining about the presence of her little sister. Paige had helped her put together her college application so that she got the place in film school she wanted. Even Morgan, so busy with her own dreams, had helped her pick out prom clothes and given her advice about boys. Truthfully, Hanna could barely think of a moment of her life when her sisters hadn't been there to make things easier for her.

Even her mother's death in the island's horrible flu epidemic two decades ago wasn't as hard for her as it had been for the others because Hanna had been so young that her sisters had gone out of their way to keep her from the worst of it. Emily, Rachel, Paige and Morgan had put aside their own grief just so that they could make things that little bit better for Hanna.

But when had Hanna last done something that was genuinely difficult? And what was worth stepping out from behind their shield of affection for? Was it all worth the pain she was feeling now?

But she already knew the answer, didn't she?

Joel was worth risking everything for.

Hanna got out her camera, positioning it so that it would film her sitting on her bed. She knew she looked terrible, with puffy eyes and tangled hair, but she didn't care. Telling him the truth was all that mattered right now, not looking pretty or attractive.

She didn't have anything planned, didn't have a script to read from, as she hit the record button. All she could do was speak from her heart.

"Joel, I know you probably won't want to play this video for too long. But I hope you'll watch long enough for me to tell you the truth. The truth about what happened...and also the truth about how I feel."

Hanna swallowed. This was harder than she had thought it would be, yet she knew she needed to keep going.

"Let's start with the truth about Poppy. It turns out that she left the island with help from my grandmother, as well as from William II. Not only did your great aunt and my grandfather not want to marry one another, but Poppy wanted to follow her dreams and write poetry, and she thought she needed to leave the island and her family to do it. But according to my grandmother,

Poppy always planned to come back once she had succeeded. Obviously, she never did. I know learning what Poppy did hurt you, and I'm so sorry about that...but I also know it would have crushed her spirit to give up her dreams."

The truth about Poppy was the easy part, though.

"Now for the truth about me." It should have been the more straightforward part—just a few simple words—yet it was anything but easy. "I love you, Joel." Her voice was shaking now, but she knew she had to get through this, knew she needed to tell him everything that was in her heart. "And I think you love me too. At least, I hope you do."

She paused again, trying to think how to phrase the next part, yet there wasn't a choice, not really. She had to keep telling the truth, even if it might cost her Joel.

"And you were right, I am planning to go back to school in Seattle...but that doesn't mean I ever planned on leaving you, too. Times are different now from the way they were when Poppy was my age and trying to follow her dreams. She believed she had to leave her family and friends so that she could become the person she wanted to be, but I know better. I know that my dreams are so much richer when the people I love are a part of them. And," she added with a small smile, "I can't help but think that if there's anyone in a position to visit me in Seattle and to pick me up to bring me back to the island, it's a man with his own fleet of ships, who also happens to love sailing them."

Hanna turned the camera off, then sent it in an email to Joel without editing out a word.

The easiest thing at this point would be to sit back and wait for a response from Joel, maybe let herself recover a little before she pressed on. But since she'd been the one to dig up his great aunt's history, Hanna knew she'd never be able to live with herself if she left the mystery unsolved and unfinished.

Picking the envelopes and postcards back up and going through them again, she saw that while they'd come from all over the country for two years, four of the postcards showed the same view and the postmark on those envelopes were from Oregon. The view looked out over a town along the coast to a very distinctive ridge.

She scanned the photograph onto her computer and set about an image search. Slowly, she started to go through the results, and when she stumbled onto a web site dedicated to old photographs from the region, she finally found what she was looking for.

All four views were from the same coastal town: Woodburn, Oregon.

Had Poppy spent time there? Had she lived there? Or had she simply been passing through? Certainly, it looked like she couldn't have been there long, since the postcards had stopped so suddenly. Or maybe the opposite was true. Maybe she'd finally settled down so much that she didn't need reminders of Walker Island.

Pushing away the thought that she'd hit another dead end, Hanna began to do some research on the town, searching for any clues that might lead her to Poppy. Her eyes were starting to blur when something finally caught Hanna's eye.

It seemed that this small town in Oregon was known for its annual poetry festival.

CHAPTER FIFTEEN

Hanna woke up the next morning to the sound of Emily's raised voice, "No, she can't come down. And why would you possibly think she'd want to see you again after what you did to her yesterday?"

Joel? Was he here to see her? But by the time Hanna threw on her robe, Emily was already shutting the door.

"Emily, wait!" Hanna called, rushing down to stop her. Sure enough, Joel was standing there outside. "Joel, I'm so glad you got the video I emailed to you!"

"You sent me a video?"

Emily looked just as surprised, and more than a little upset, as well. Hanna put her hand on her sister's arm. "Thank you for protecting me, but I need to speak with Joel. Alone."

Emily looked at her for a long moment before finally nodding. Still, she said, "Just holler if you need one of us to throw him out for you."

"No. I won't want that." Finally, Emily headed back into the kitchen, leaving Hanna and Joel standing together on the doorstep.

"You really didn't get the video?" Hanna asked.

Joel shook his head. And now that she looked at him more carefully, she realized he didn't really look like someone who had come back to declare their undying love. In fact, he still looked fairly upset, almost the way he had back in Seattle.

Just the thought of their conversation on the B&B porch was enough to bring a fresh pang of pain to Hanna, but she forced herself to hide it away as she asked, "Then why are you here?"

"We started this documentary of yours together and I think we need to finish it together."

It wasn't a declaration of love—not anywhere close to it, actually—but the fact that he was here standing on her doorstep wanting to continue working with her to unravel the mystery of what really happened to his great aunt felt important.

"Actually, that's part of what I needed to tell you in the video I emailed to you. Come inside, Joel. Please."

For a moment, she thought Joel might not do it, but when he walked in then said, "I believe this will mark the first time a Peterson has been inside a Walker home for more than six decades," she wanted to leap for joy.

Everything couldn't be completely lost if he

was teasing her with their special joke, could it?

"I found out more about Poppy," Hanna said once she'd closed the front door behind them. "My grandmother told me what happened."

Joel stared at her, barely blinking. "Tell me."

"Grams says that Poppy told her straight to her face that she never loved William II. What she wanted more than anything was to be a poet, but she feared she'd never get the chance if she remained here following her family's plans for her life. Grams also said that Poppy always intended to come back home after she'd made a name for herself as a poet." A muscle jumped in Joel's jaw as if he couldn't let himself believe that part, and Hanna wanted so badly to convince him that it was true. Hopefully, they'd learn something soon that would prove it to Joel in a way he wouldn't be able to deny. "I get the feeling that Grams and Poppy became pretty good friends in the time they knew each other. At least, Poppy kept sending her postcards for two years."

"Why wouldn't your grandmother have said anything to let my family know Poppy was okay?"

"She made Poppy a promise, Joel, and swore she wouldn't break it. When Grams makes a promise, she really keeps it."

"Then why would she have finally broken it now?"

Hanna refused to look away from his beautiful eyes. "For us."

And for love.

But she could see that he wasn't yet ready to

talk about their relationship—or how everything beautiful could have gone wrong so fast—so she turned the focus back to his great aunt. "Based on the box of postcards that Grams kept, I now know where Poppy went after Seattle. It was a small town, down near Portland, called Woodburn."

"Are you sure?"

"I am. Especially since I found out that the town is renowned for its poetry festival."

"Then what are we waiting for?"

She stared at him in surprise. "You want to go there? Now? With me?"

"Like I said, we began this together, and I think we should end it together, too."

She hated the way he spoke of endings, but at least she would get one more day with him as they travelled to Oregon. And maybe, she hoped, that would be enough time for him to realize he cared about her as much as she cared about him and that together they could find a way to make things work out between them.

Even if he was a Peterson who lived on the island...and she was a Walker studying at the University in Seattle.

* * *

Fifteen minutes later, as they were boarding the ferry, Hanna took out her cell phone and placed a call to the president of Woodburn's local poetry society, whose name and number she had found on their web site during her online research the previous evening.

"Hello, Ms. Stevens? My name's Hanna Walker. I understand you're the president of the poetry society?"

"If this is about getting your poetry into our newsletter, the deadline has already passed."

"No, that's not why I'm calling," Hanna assured her quickly. "I'm actually looking for information on a poet who might have visited your festival a while ago, probably in the early 1950s."

"The 1950s?" Ms. Stevens was clearly stunned by Hanna's request. "Why on Earth are you searching for a poet who might have passed through here more than six decades ago?"

Hanna tried to explain about her documentary as simply as she could, though even leaving out most of the finer details of what had happened on Walker Island so long ago, she was speaking for quite a while. Finally, she closed with, "Poppy's great nephew and I both need to find out what happened to her. I know it's a long shot, but we at least have to try."

"My family means a great deal to me, too," Ms. Stevens said after a long enough pause that Hanna nearly wondered if she'd hung up during her long explanation, "and if someone had disappeared along the way, I'd want to find them, too. I'll give you my address and you can come on over anytime you're ready."

"How about today? In say, three hours?"

"Three hours? Wouldn't that mean you're already on your way?"

"We are."

Hanna knew it probably seemed a little crazy, going all the way to Portland and beyond, just on the off chance of finding another small clue about Poppy's whereabouts. Yet, they needed to do this. Not just because of the documentary, but because she and Joel both needed to see this through, regardless of where it took them.

Joel had been quiet the whole time she was speaking on the phone and now, as they drove off the ferry and headed through downtown Seattle, past the street with the B&B that held so many memories both for them and his great aunt, Hanna could feel him tensing up beside her. Slowly though, as they left the city behind and headed south on the freeway toward Oregon, he began to relax, even smiling a little as the sun came out once they were on the I-5. They didn't talk much about anything important during the three hour drive, but knowing that soon enough they might be facing more difficult revelations, Hanna simply appreciated the chance to be with Joel again.

* * *

Ms. Stevens, or Justine as she quickly reintroduced herself, was a pleasant woman in her mid-forties. Her home was so full of books that at first glance it seemed as if the walls were being held up by the stacks of them, and finding a place to sit involved moving aside at least a couple piles of books. So did setting up Hanna's camera, which Justine said she had no problem with at all.

"So, you're looking for someone named Poppy Peterson, who might have visited us in the fifties?" When Hanna nodded, the other woman sighed. "You realize that the odds of finding one person who visited a poetry festival wouldn't be good, even if that festival were just a year or two back? Sixty years...I just keep worrying that you'll have ended up wasting your time if we can't find anything."

But since Hanna had gotten to spend the day with Joel, no matter what they did or didn't find out about Poppy, it definitely hadn't been a wasted trip.

"In the B&B in Seattle, she used another name so that no one in the family could trace her to bring her home," Joel said. "Penny P. was what she called herself." Reaching into his pocket, he put Poppy's final poem onto the coffee table between them. "Hopefully, seeing this might help. It's the poem my great aunt left behind when she disappeared."

Hanna put the photo of Poppy and Ava beside the note. "This is her, on the right. The other woman is my grandmother."

Justine looked back and forth between the photograph and the poem several times when suddenly, it was as if a light bulb switched on inside of her. She stood up animatedly, heading over to the stacks of books and searching through them so quickly that Hanna briefly wondered if they were all about to come tumbling down in a literary avalanche.

"I didn't recognize the name, of course, but as you guessed, Poppy Peterson wasn't the name she published under. It wasn't Penny, either. To everyone back in the fifties, she was Pansy Pendleton. She wasn't one of the big names of the beat generation," Justine said as she handed them a slim leather bound book, "but she did spend plenty of time down in San Francisco. There are some people, and I'm one of them, who think that she helped to influence Ginsburg."

"Poppy was famous?" Hanna asked.

"She was definitely starting to get there," Justine said with a nod. "The other poets of the time knew who she was and admired her. I believe when she came to our festival that she was working her way up from San Francisco, stopping in small towns to meet with other poets along the way. Apparently, she was planning to stay here around a week, for the event, and then keep moving north. But—" Justine's excited expression fell away. "One day she was out swimming in the ocean, the next she was in her sickbed with pneumonia. A couple of days after that...I'm sorry, I know how hard it must be to hear this."

"It's better than not knowing," Joel said.

"Well," Justine said gently, "your great aunt passed away, and it was such a tragic loss. Who knows what she might have done if that hadn't happened?"

She might have gone home, Hanna thought. She couldn't prove it, but something in her heart told her she was right. Poppy had left the island for a while to pursue her dreams, just the way Hanna had for filmmaking school, but she'd never planned on leaving forever.

Hanna reached into her bag for the envelopes and postcards Grams had given her. She'd already arranged them in date order, but now she began to set them out, getting out her phone and pulling up a map to look at the postmarks.

"What are you doing?" Joel asked.

"Plotting her route," Hanna explained.

It was fairly easy now that she knew what had happened. The early ones worked their way down the coast, bit by bit, to San Francisco. Some headed east, probably pointing to adventures or trips away from the city. For the last few, though, there was a definite sequence. Sacramento, Redding, Roseburg...always heading north.

"She was coming back, Joel." Her chest clenched at the sure knowledge that Poppy hadn't meant to leave her family behind. "She was coming back to Walker Island."

Joel stared at the map Hanna had made with the postcards for a long while before he finally nodded. "She was," he agreed. "She was coming home."

He closed his eyes, rubbing a hand over them in obvious exhaustion. In Seattle, he'd been so convinced that Poppy had just abandoned everyone. Even when Grams had told Hanna that she'd gone off to follow her dream, it had still seemed selfish the way Poppy had left and never looked back.

But she *had* looked back. She had even tried to come back. At least until simple chance—and bad luck—had robbed her of that last homecoming.

There was only one question left to ask. But Joel beat Hanna to it.

"Where is she buried?"

CHAPTER SIXTEEN

When Hanna had first walked into his office, Joel never thought that it would lead to him standing in front of his great aunt's grave in Woodburn, Oregon. He'd been so certain that she'd deliberately died at sea, and that Hanna was wasting everyone's time. But then, after their trip to Seattle, there had been some small part of him wondering if she might still be out there somewhere, still avoiding the family she had left all those years ago. Perhaps with another family, a new one that knew nothing of the family she'd left behind on Walker Island.

Now, though, he'd finally found her. And only because of Hanna.

Still, it was strange to stare at the tombstone and read the name Pansy Pendleton, rather than Poppy Peterson. She'd had such a short life, yet it seemed like the part where she'd really lived her dreams had been as someone else. Only to be struck down suddenly, just as she was finally reaching her goals.

Could he bring her home, he wondered? And even if he could find a way, should he bring her back to Walker Island and complete that journey for her? Would that be the right end to all of this? She'd been trying to get home to her family, but it wasn't like there was really much of her family left for her there. Bringing her back might complete her last journey, but was it the right thing to do?

"Are you doing okay?"

Hanna had put a hand over his and Joel realized that for once, she didn't have her camera out. Instead of looking through the camera's lens at the world, every inch of her was focused on him.

"Why aren't you filming? Don't you want to finish your documentary?"

"This is too private."

"But if you don't include this part, then how is the world going to know who Pansy Pendleton really was? They deserve to know the truth, and Poppy...well, I'd like to think she'd want it too."

"Are you sure?"

He looked into Hanna's eyes and the warmth—and the love—he saw in the clear blue depths made it even easier to say, "I'm sure. Completely sure."

As she started to set up her camera, Joel knew that when she finished editing her documentary, it was going to be spectacular. He had never met anyone so passionate about her art, who was so good, so natural, at what she did. There was no question whatsoever that Hanna would secure her place in the master's program and soon be leaving the island for Seattle again.

But now, strangely, that thought didn't bring with it the same deep sense of betrayal and dread it had back at the B&B. After all, although Poppy had left, Hanna and her postcards had proved to him that she'd been on her way back.

Did he really want to push Hanna away just because he was afraid that she might leave the island and never come back? Especially when even just one night without her had proved to him just how empty his life felt without her in it.

"Hanna," he said. "About Seattle…"

Her video camera was already pointed at him as she told him, "We don't have to talk about that now, Joel."

"Yes, we do. I shouldn't have done what I did, shouldn't have said what I said. I was so caught up in what had happened in the past that I couldn't see what was right in front of me."

Hanna leaned away from her camera, her eyes widened in surprise. "I was too caught up with my story to stop to think how much it might hurt you. I'm sorry, Joel. You're the last person I would ever want to hurt."

"I know you never wanted to hurt me, Hanna. And you haven't."

There was so much more he wanted to say, so much he needed to say, but when he opened his mouth to speak, he realized there was nothing that he could say that would put right what had happened in the past. Nothing that could undo it all.

"It's okay, Joel," Hanna said again, "we don't have to do this right now. If you want me to stop filming, I will."

"No, don't stop," he told her. Because it wasn't okay. And it hadn't been okay for sixty years. "I never met Poppy, but she was always there like a ghost haunting my family, haunting me. When I was a kid, one of the first things I can remember my parents doing is telling me the story of how William Walker II hurt Poppy so much that she killed herself and that I should stay away from your family, no matter what. All those years at school, and I barely said a word to a Walker because of something that happened decades ago."

It wasn't just at the school, though, and it wasn't just he and Hanna and her sisters who had been affected. How many people on the island had been pushed into taking one side or the other, with the people who worked on the Peterson boats being careful about just how friendly they became with the island's 'other' family? And then, of course, there was the way he'd pushed Hanna away again and again because he thought he was supposed to uphold family loyalty.

"I'm sorry for all the years I ignored you and your sisters. This all started with a wedding that didn't happen. Of the people involved, only one is still alive, and I've spent so much time blaming Ava for all of this when I shouldn't have. All she did was fall in love with your grandfather and be a good enough friend to Poppy to keep her secrets. I need to apologize to her, too."

"Something tells me that Grams doesn't need you to do that. She knows none of this is anyone's fault, especially yours," Hanna said. "Honestly, I think just the fact that people know the truth now will be enough."

Joel hadn't thought he would feel this much at the grave of a woman he had never known, but he'd known the *idea* of Poppy all his life. And now it turned out that idea of her had been completely wrong.

It had taken Hanna to show him the reality behind all the stories he'd been told. She had such a gift for finding the truth. And for showing it to people. She had the ability to look at the world in new ways, and because she was doing it through her video camera, it made everyone else look at things differently too.

"When you started this, Hanna, I was convinced that you weren't going to tell the whole story. I thought that you were going to tell a version of what had happened that was so far from what we all knew to be true that it would be unrecognizable. And the truth is, you did. But not for the reasons I thought. Not because you're a Walker trying to make your family look better, but because it's the truth, and the truth needed to finally be told. Your grandmother and grandfather endured decades of unpleasantness and malicious gossip just to help out my great aunt. I know there will be people on the island who won't want to believe what we've found out together, but they should, because for the first time..." Joel paused and looked back at Poppy's gravestone. "For the first time, I feel like this is finally settled."

He tried visualizing Poppy's face, and every time he did, it blended and blurred with Hanna's in his mind.

They were so similar in so many ways. So artistic, and so driven. His great aunt had been willing to put aside all the advantages and security that her family name had given her on the island to reach for her dream, and she'd had the strength to stay away until she achieved it. It must have taken a lot of determination, and so much courage, for Poppy to leave the island to pursue her poetry writing. Just as it had taken determination and courage for Hanna to pursue her documentary about their families despite every roadblock in her way.

Yet, she'd known when to stop, too, when she'd offered not to film this part—the most important part of all—just because she didn't want to hurt him.

"What are you thinking?" Hanna asked, moving to stand beside him, her camera off now.

"I was thinking that Poppy reminds me of you, that it must have been hard for her to do what she did, and that you're both such strong, incredible women to have the courage to follow your dreams, no matter what." He reached for her hand, letting her natural warmth heat up all the places inside of him that had been cold for so long.

"Before we left Justine's house," Hanna told him in a soft voice, "she said that they still get people visiting the grave. Pansy Pendleton might not have been famous, exactly, but she definitely inspired people."

Pansy Pendleton. It wasn't a name Joel could get used to, but it had been who Poppy was at the end. More importantly, it had been who she *wanted* to be. Poppy had been too tied down by the expectations of the Peterson family, but Pansy could be a poet.

What right did Joel really have to take her back to the island? This was where her dreams had led her. This was where people still remembered her for the things she wanted to be remembered for.

Finally, he did what he'd wanted to do every second since this morning, and drew Hanna into his arms. "What did you say on the video you emailed me? All day long, I've been dying to know."

Hanna looked up at him, so lovely that she took his breath away. "You know what I said, Joel."

And the truth was that he did.

"I love you too." He leaned down to kiss her,

but before he did, he had to say, "And that's most definitely the first time a Peterson has *ever* said that to a Walker."

CHAPTER SEVENTEEN

The B&B they stayed at that night had several rooms available, but they only needed the one this time. Still, even though they'd both confessed their love to each other, Hanna knew they'd have plenty to work out along the way. Now, however, she knew for sure that they'd find a way to be together. As for her family, well, hopefully they'd be able to accept that Hanna was in love with Joel, and that he was in love with her.

The next morning, Hanna left Joel in bed still sleeping. After everything he'd learned the past few days, she wasn't surprised that he was exhausted. She took her camera and laptop downstairs to breakfast so that she could start editing together some of the footage while she could still remember all the feelings involved.

In the first shots she'd gotten of Joel back in his office, right at the start of all this, he looked good, of course, but she was struck by the way there seemed to be something different about him now.

Last night, he'd seemed more at peace. Had finding out about his great aunt's past done that?

Or was it falling in love with her?

Systematically, she spliced together the footage she'd shot, but all the while, she couldn't help feeling that it wasn't completely right.

Knowing she often hit on inspiration when she stepped away from her computer, she got up to clear her head for a few minutes. All around the B&B, there were framed pictures and pieces of writing on the wall, most of them from the poetry festival.

A few minutes later, Hanna stopped, shocked, in front of one of the poems. She had to read it twice before she grabbed her things, then ran back up the stairs to get Joel.

He was just coming out of their room when she reached him and took his hand. "There's something you've got to see downstairs. Trust me, Joel, it's amazing."

"Of course I trust you."

She'd been in such a hurry to take him downstairs, but now, she had to stop to press a kiss to his beautiful mouth. Having his trust meant the world to her.

When they finally pulled apart, Hanna led the way through to the dining room and pointed to the frame with one hand, holding on to his hand with the other.

"It's one of Poppy's poems." Joel sounded as

stunned as she'd felt when she saw it a few minutes earlier. "*The Way Home* by Pansy Pendleton," he said, his voice warm and strong and full of emotion as he read the short, but beautiful poem about tides turning back to the familiar sands of home aloud.

A short while later he said, "It's beautiful, but the writing style isn't quite the same as her last poem from the island, is it?"

"Poppy had been working seriously at her craft for two years by the time she wrote this, so I suppose it isn't surprising that the style is a bit different," Hanna suggested. "But the images and the ideas about forging new paths and dreams...doesn't it feel like this poem is almost a sequel to the one she wrote when she left the island?"

"You're right. It's like that one is the beginning and this one is the end."

The inn's owner, a man in his forties with slightly thinning hair who had an amazing knack of balancing half a dozen breakfast plates at once, stopped beside the two of them.

"Ah, I see you're interested in Pansy Pendleton's last poem."

"Her *last* poem?" Hanna asked.

"It's why it's up on the wall," the inn's owner explained. "She wrote it here, and I believe she was planning to read it at the poetry festival. But Justine is the expert on all of this. Have you met Justine?"

Hanna nodded, knowing both she and Joel

owed the head of the Woodburn Poetry Society more than they could say. Without her, they never would have worked out Pansy Pendleton's real identity and learned what happened to Poppy.

"I was thinking," Joel said as he turned to her, "that perhaps I might let the Poetry Society here have Poppy's old journals and poetry as a thank you. I think it's time the world knew who Pansy Pendleton was, that she was also Poppy Peterson, and that she was a brave woman who risked so much to follow her dreams. Do you want to come down to Justine's place and tell her with me? I'm sure it will be fun to film her reaction."

It probably would, but Hanna knew that she could go on collecting new footage forever, and never actually get her documentary finished. "I think I'd better stay here and work on editing. You don't mind, do you?"

Joel kissed her, tenderly. "You'll still be here when I come back. That's all I need to know."

Settling back into a corner of the Inn's dining room, she concentrated again on piecing her film together. But when there still seemed to be things missing, on a whim, Hanna put in some of the footage she'd taken of the whales on the ferry over to the island. The sequence shouldn't have worked, because it took the focus away from the main story, yet somehow, it did.

Because wasn't the island a defining part of *her* story, too? Hanna Walker wouldn't be Hanna Walker without the island, or her sisters, or Joel and the Petersons. Joel had asked her once if she was only telling other people's stories, or if she was trying to tell her own, as well. Now she finally understood that the heart of the story she wanted to tell now, and for the rest of her life as a filmmaker, was one of love—for others, for oneself, and for dreams.

So she added in the footage of the whales, making a note to add narration about the importance of the whale migrations to the island, but also about how she'd watched the whales with awe so many times as a child. She put in footage of the storm on the northern bluffs of Walker Island where she and Joel had come so close to kissing. She put in footage of the festival and the B&B in Seattle where she'd learned he truly respected her filmmaking skills. She even included footage taken from the dance recital so that she could show her love for her sisters and Ava.

And what she found was that her documentary worked so much better when she brought herself—and her real life on the island—in. Meanwhile, she also tried to tell Joel's story alongside that of his family, although by the end, their stories were so intertwined it was hard to tell which was which.

By the time Joel walked into the room, she felt that it was almost all there. But there was still something missing. Some piece she couldn't quite see.

He lowered his mouth to hers to give her a

kiss before asking, "Can I see what you've got so far?"

She was a little nervous about showing it to him, but he smiled as he watched it, even during the more emotional sections. "It's fantastic, Hanna."

"It's really just a rough draft. There will be a lot more work to do before it's really finished. And the ending still isn't quite right somehow, leaving things in the graveyard. Maybe I should have gone with you to see Justine today."

"No, you were right to stay here, to work on your documentary while everything was so fresh. Besides, I have a better idea for the ending."

"You do?"

"I do."

The next thing she knew, he was getting down on one knee and taking a box from his pocket.

"How about with some footage of what the island has been waiting for all these years? A Peterson-Walker wedding."

"Oh my gosh." He opened the box to display a stunning antique wedding ring. "Joel, it's beautiful. Where did you get it?"

"It was Poppy's. When I showed up today, Justine said she was so glad that I came back. She remembered the ring after we left yesterday, and told me that the Poetry Society had been keeping it in a safe all this time because they couldn't locate any of her relatives. They could have never found us if we hadn't come looking for her,

Hanna. I know this documentary will secure your place in the graduate program in Seattle, because no one has ever deserved it more, but I was hoping this might give you a reason to come back once you've earned your degree."

"You've already given me all the reasons I could ever need." Still, for as much as Hanna wanted to yell *yes!* to his proposal, something wasn't quite right about this ending...and she thought she knew what it was.

Lowering herself to her knees in front of him so that they were eye to eye, she said, "I love you, Joel, so much that I can't stand the thought of your not being happy. Truly happy. If it's working in an office all day, I'll be behind you every step of the way. But I can't help but feel that you've pushed away your own dreams for too long. Far too long."

He stared at her for a long moment, before he finally nodded. "All day, I've been thinking about what Poppy went through, about how she was brave enough to pursue her dreams even though it meant disappointing our family. For so long, I thought I needed to be what they wanted me to be to keep everyone happy, even after my father and grandfather passed away. Especially then, because I didn't want to do anything that would diminish what they'd built on the island with Peterson Shipping. But now...how would you feel if your husband made his living as a sea captain?"

She threw her arms around him in answer. "I love you, Joel."

"I love you, too, Hanna. Say you'll marry me. Before or after you graduate from the master's program—it doesn't matter when or where as long as we'll be together for the rest of our lives."

"Yes." Finally she was able to shout it out. "*Yes!*"

And when he slid the ring onto her finger, she was hardly surprised by how well it fit. As endings for her documentary went, she had to admit, their wedding would be a good one.

Really, really good.

CHAPTER EIGHTEEN

They held the wedding outside so that everyone on the island could be a part of the celebration that would end the long-running feud between the Petersons and the Walkers. Hanna had set up cameras all over the beach to capture the celebration for her documentary, and fortunately, everyone had offered to pitch in on all other fronts for the huge wedding and party.

Emily had insisted on taking over the catering for the event, baking and cooking with such intensity that Hanna had almost been worried that her sister didn't approve of her and Joel. Of course, Emily had quickly dispelled that by saying, "I don't just cook when I'm annoyed, you know." She'd hugged Hanna, then. "I'm happy for you. We all are."

Paige had co-opted a few of her students from the dance school into volunteering to pitch in for the occasion. Hanna had been a little worried about whether that was allowed, but Paige had laughed it off.

"Are you kidding? Most of them would kill for a chance to be involved in the island's biggest wedding."

"It's not *that* big," Hanna insisted. "It's not like we're putting on some sort of elaborate, over-the-top show."

"Only because the two of you didn't give us enough time to set that up. A month isn't nearly enough time to plan a wedding, Hanna. Although," Paige said with a twinkle in her eyes, "watching the way you and Joel are together, I can understand why you don't want to waste another moment."

They'd wanted to get married before she headed back to the university. Not only had her official acceptance into the graduate program come through, but Professor Karlson had even been talking about showing it to a couple of production company friends of his.

Still, for as happy as all of that made her, in the end, getting into graduate school and impressing her professor wasn't really the point.

The point was that it was the story of Hanna's heart that she had needed to tell.

And now, all she needed to do was walk up the aisle, or at least the patch of beach that counted as the aisle for today, on the north side of the island near the caves where she and Joel had taken refuge from the storm. Right this moment, in fact, she was using the cave where they'd sheltered to get ready, with her sister Morgan fussing with Hanna's dress and makeup, applying a little eye shadow. Morgan coming back home for the wedding so that all five sisters could be together again made the day even better than it already was.

"When did you get the pink highlights, Hanna?"

"A while ago. Do you think they don't suit me?"

"Hanna, it's your wedding day. Everything suits you." Morgan hugged her. "Although, honestly, I'm still trying to get my head around you and Joel Peterson. We haven't had a chance to talk much, but from the little we have I really like him. Still, I never would have thought..."

"Me neither," Hanna told her with a smile. "I guess you never know how these things are going to turn out."

"No, I guess not," Morgan agreed.

Like Hanna's other sisters, Morgan had decided not to wear a formal bridesmaid's dress. Instead, she was wearing a butter-yellow dress that floated like waves around her kneecaps.

"You do realize that with our little sister getting married, you've just managed to make the rest of us feel old? Even those of us who are just a couple of years older than you?"

Hanna grinned and teased, "Yet another good reason to get married as soon as possible."

Morgan returned her grin. "No, that would be the part where you love Joel with all your heart."

"I really do, Morgan. He's *amazing*."

"In that case, I think it's time for you to go get married."

Hanna paused, savoring the heady moment, before stepping out onto the path down to the beach. It was a slightly trickier climb down in a wedding dress, but the extra time it took meant that she got a better look at all the people gathered down below on the beach on the chairs set up just above the tide line.

Ava sat down in the front row, and Hanna could see her already dabbing at her eyes. Every seat was taken, and people were also gathered on every last bit of beach. There were even watchers on the sea.

For today, amazingly, all of the captains and skippers from Peterson shipping were out in the waters just beyond the beach in support of Joel. Just last week, he'd formally announced that he would be hiring a general manager to handle the day-to-day business, giving him more time out on the boats, and they'd all rallied behind their boss, who loved the sea just as much as they did.

Joel was waiting for her by the small arch that Michael had helped put up on the beach for the ceremony, staring at her in wonder as she began her approach. He looked amazing standing there, gorgeous in his tux, though very definitely not wearing a tie. Hanna had insisted on that part.

Her father, Tres, was there beside Ava. Hanna knew he'd gotten the shock of his life when he'd come back from his European school trip to find his little girl was engaged to Joel Peterson. Thankfully, Ava had quickly and deftly explained the situation to him, with Hanna's sisters there, as well, to confirm that Joel really was Hanna's dream come true...and that he loved her with his entire heart and soul, as well.

Having every eye on her was a strange feeling when she was usually the one watching everyone else. For today, though, she could accept being the center of attention, especially when there was only one gaze that mattered.

Everything but Joel fell away when he looked at her with so much love and heat in his eyes that it stole her breath. So when the officiant started the ceremony, it almost took her by surprise.

"We're gathered here to witness the marriage of..."

As he spoke, Hanna couldn't help thinking of everything it had taken to get here today. All those decades when their families hadn't spoken. All the gossip that had been spread about her grandmother. She thought about herself growing up without a mother, but with so much love from her sisters, father and grandmother. And she thought about Joel, too—the way the teenage boy she'd had a girlhood crush on, who had so deftly darted through the defenses of opposing football teams, had become the incredible man who stood opposite her now, holding her hand and waiting for her to say the two words that would bind them together forever.

"I do."

* * *

They held the wedding reception up at the house and, to Hanna, it looked almost as busy as a downtown Seattle festival. There was music playing loud enough that it could be heard outside, and food was set out on every available surface. Rachel was off at one side of the room chatting with friends while keeping an eye on Charlotte as she ran around excitedly with a couple of the island's younger children. Paige was dancing, while Emily was making sure everyone had what they needed. Morgan, of course, had attracted a small group of admirers interested in hearing about her adventures in Hollywood.

But it was Ava whom Hanna and Joel sought out. Hanna's grandmother hugged her first, squeezing her tightly. "You have made me the happiest I've ever been, darling."

Beside Hanna, Joel smiled. "I'm pretty pleased too."

Ava pulled Joel into an embrace that looked stronger than her age might have suggested. "I know Poppy would be proud of you, both of you."

"I know she would too, Ava, and I'm sorry that for so long I thought—"

"Oh, hush now," Ava said in a gentle voice. "Must we go through this every time I see you? I'm just happy for the two of you. And you should know that if my granddaughter doesn't wear you out too much first, young man, I'm going to be claiming a dance from you later."

As Ava stepped away, Hanna told her new

husband, "She's serious about the dance, you know."

"Then we'd better get some practice in first," Joel suggested.

Putting their arms around one another, they swayed in time to the music. Joel, she already knew, was a fabulous dancer, and long after the song ended, they remained in each other's arms.

Finally, however, they had to pull apart for the speeches as Ava began to speak into the portable microphone that Emily handed her. "I know many of you would like to toast Hanna and Joel today, because they're truly wonderful together and it means so much to all of us to have this wedding after all this time. I'd like to begin the toasts by saying thank you to both of them for giving me a truly wonderful gift. Not only a radiantly happy granddaughter and a new grandson-in-law that I couldn't be prouder of, but they also gave me back a friend I thought I had lost, along with the truth." Focusing her loving gaze on Hanna and Joel, she said, "We all love you and wish you every happiness."

Everyone joined in the toast with cheers and clinking glasses of champagne. And for the next thirty minutes, with Joel's arms tight around her waist, Hanna rested her head on his chest and together they listened to their family and friends' beautiful toasts.

As soon as the toasts were over and Joel had taken Ava for a spin around the dance floor, Hanna's new husband was quick to pull her into his arms and suggest, "I'm thinking that we should take a page from my great aunt's book."

"Running off to the big city to seek our fortunes?" Hanna asked.

"I'm thinking more along the lines of seeing if anyone notices if we slip away."

"And miss the rest of the party?"

Joel kissed her, then said, "I think Poppy, William and Ava all understood that weddings are often for other people. But being married...that part's for us."

Hanna looked around. Joel had a point. The party had reached that stage where everyone was having a perfectly good time without them.

"I guess we *could* always catch the rest on the wedding videos."

EPILOGUE

Morgan smiled as she watched her sister and Joel slip out of the party. Even though the wedding had been so sudden, she suspected that they were going to be perfect together.

She was glad that she'd been able to get back for the wedding, even if it had taken a last minute flight on a jet belonging to the star of the movie she was working on. And as soon as the ceremony had ended, Morgan had found herself at the center of a small group of young women who clearly wished that they were the ones who had her career.

"What was it like working on your last movie?" one asked. "Is it true what I heard about you and Bradley Lewis?"

"Bradley is a wonderful man," Morgan said about the leading man on the last movie she'd worked on, "but you have to remember that you shouldn't believe the things you read in magazines. He's happily married, and the two of us are *definitely* not involved."

"I wish he'd kiss *me,* though," one of the girls said, before her friend asked, "Can I get your autograph?"

Morgan knew she ought to break up the little clique of...well, they weren't exactly fans. They were just girls who found even the dimly reflected glory of moviemaking spectacular. Morgan knew how that went, and ordinarily, she did her best to be accommodating when people treated her like a minor celebrity. But this wasn't the time and the place. She wanted to go catch up with her other sisters, and she wanted to play with Charlotte, who had grown so much since the last time she was back on the island.

But at the same time, she'd been so worried all day about seeing Brian Russell again that she'd done her best to stay on the fringes of things. He'd been her boyfriend in high school and in the seven years since their breakup, she hadn't spoken to him or seen him again. Not even once.

Today, the crowd watching the wedding had been so big—and she'd been so focused on Hanna during the ceremony—that she hadn't caught sight of him out on the beach. Later, during the reception, she swore she'd felt her skin tingle and grow warm the way it always had when he'd looked at her, but Brian was nowhere to be found, and she figured it was just her overactive imagination kicking in.

She supposed he was probably avoiding the

Peterson-Walker celebration on her account, and she tried to convince herself that he was right to do just that. Because what would happen if she did suddenly see him again, face to face for the first time in seven years? Would sparks fly again the way they always had? Would she be unable to stop herself from going up to him to ask him to kiss her the way he once had, with so much passion that it had made her head spin?

And next month, when she temporarily returned to the island to work on her new organic makeup line, how were they going to keep their distance from each other for more than just one day? What was she going to do if it turned out that she was as drawn to Brian now as she'd been back in high school when they were sweethearts?

Morgan worked to shake the troublesome thoughts and questions out of her head. Today was one of the happiest days for her family in recent memory and she was going to do her best to forget about Brian and enjoy it to the fullest before she had to get back on a plane to New York City tomorrow morning.

~ THE END ~

ABOUT THE AUTHOR

When New York Times and USA Today bestseller Lucy Kevin released her first novel, SEATTLE GIRL, it became an instant bestseller. All of her subsequent sweet contemporary romances have been hits with readers as well, including WHEN IT'S LOVE (A Walker Island Romance, Book 3) which debuted at #1. Having been called "One of the top writers in America" by The Washington Post, she recently launched the very romantic Walker Island series. Lucy also writes contemporary romances as Bella Andre and her incredibly popular series about The Sullivans have been #1 bestsellers around the world, with more than 4 million books sold so far! If not behind her computer, you can find her swimming, hiking or laughing with her husband and two children. For a complete listing of books, as well as excerpts, contests, and to connect with Lucy please visit www.LucyKevin.com.

Made in the USA
San Bernardino, CA
26 April 2016